mini S·A·G·A·S·

Kent

First published in Great Britain in 2007 by
Young Writers, Remus House, Coltsfoot Drive,
Peterborough, PE2 9JX
Tel (01733) 890066 Fax (01733) 313524
All Rights Reserved

© Copyright Contributors 2007
SB ISBN 978-1-84431-341-9

Foreword

Young Writers was established in 1991, with the aim of encouraging the children and young adults of today to think and write creatively. Our latest secondary school competition, 'Mini S.A.G.A.S.', posed an exciting challenge for these young authors: to write, in no more than fifty words, a story encompassing a beginning, a middle and an end.
We call this the mini saga.

Mini S.A.G.A.S. Kent is our latest offering from the wealth of young talent that has mastered this incredibly challenging form. With such an abundance of imagination, humour and ability evident in such a wide variety of stories, these young writers cannot fail to enthral and excite with every tale.

Contents

The Mini Sagas

Paradise

I was in the best place ever, better than being in paradise. Deserted beaches with white sands and blue seas. Better than the best love anyone could ever feel. I was sweating from the palms and face and then I woke up and dreamt on.

Rebecca (17)

Fate

I was trapped in a box; eyes glowered down on me from all directions. I tried to move, but snake-like objects restrained me: 'Hang on;' I could hear muffled voices; staring into dark pools. I must have looked panic-stricken. I heard it; my fate was decided, 'Not guilty.'

Abby Taylor-Baptie (12)
Barton Court Grammar School

Warpath

Our movement, slow. Our visibility, poor. We trudged through the forest, men were picked off by bombs. Ground, sludge-like and cold. A rustling then a huge beast mauled my squadron. A yell. 'Billy, pick up your toys and get the dog in! No dawdling, I'm on the warpath today!'

Jordan Board (11)
Barton Court Grammar School

The Monster

It came towards me baring its white teeth. I walked back and fell onto my bed. It came nearer with blue legs and a green chest. It was shouting at me. I closed my eyes and wished it wouldn't come nearer. It came into my room. It was my brother.

Lena Dalton (12)
Barton Court Grammar School

18

The Beckoning Waters

Panting with terror, she stood by the edge, the cool mesmerising water lapping her feet. Tentatively, she shuffled forward and a surge of water washed over her feet. Desperately scrabbling back, she turned and fled, stumbling wildly in her horror-struck charge. 'Coward!' called her friends in the swimming pool.

Beverley Newing (14)
Barton Court Grammar School

Sea Of Colour

Entering the ever moving waterfall, the cascade
of colours blinding me, the ever-changing patterns
moving, swirling, the wave like motion making me
sea-sick, my retinas burning in the light.
I tore my eye from the kaleidoscope.

Eva Waffis (14)
Barton Court Grammar School

Angel

I was flying. I looked at my shiny halo and my glorious
white wings. I felt the breeze as I soared high.
'Heaven! Here I come!' I soared up at high speed.
I saw Heaven's gates getting closer. My head glided
through the cloud. I was hit by an aeroplane …

Christian Foxley (14)
Barton Court Grammar School

21

YoungWriters

The Truth

I sat with my mum. We were watching a chat TV
show. 'Mum?' I asked.
'Wait,' she said 'until the adverts.'
'But Mum!'
She gave me a glance. The advertisements eventually
came.
'Those silly girls getting pregnant so young!' she said
sadly. I looked at her tearfully. 'Now what's wrong?'

Kymberley Tan (14)
Barton Court Grammar School

Time

Perched on the edge, getting ready for the jump,
it was almost time. With the sun shining down, the
bright colours glittered in the light. 'One, two, three
- go!' Almost reaching the floor - before, with a pull,
the yo-yo returned back to the hand once more.

Georgia Toms (14)
Barton Court Grammar School

Monster Of The Deep

I dragged myself out of the murky pond. 'Phew, it's over.'
I was safe from the dark monster that was swimming and stalking in the pond; so was my wife. We ran back towards the caravan, soaked through to the bone.
Then I remembered, 'Damn, I have forgotten the kids.'

Daniel Myhill (14)
Barton Court Grammar School

24

Life

The boy strolled down the street, taking in the vibrant colours of life. He stepped onto the road to cross just as soon as a car thundered down the street; too fast to stop. The boy only stared as it hit him with ultimate force.

'Not again,' the ghost said.

Max Coleman (13)
Barton Court Grammar School

Supernatural

Shrouded in darkness, the world went black, drowning in the void. I was afraid to look, knowing if I did, I'd see nothing. Not seeing meant not knowing. Things lurked in the darkness - I'd heard the stories. Vampires, werewolves, hateful beings both time and beauty had forgotten. The eclipse ended.

Faye Wiffs (14)
Barton Court Grammar School

Haunted

A girl walked in, sweat rolling down her forehead, hair soaked. She carried a knife in her hand. The lightning cracked outside and the window swung open. It was dark. They heard an evil laugh. A scream.

'Wow Kat! The haunted house was wicked!'

Marya Muzart (12)
Barton Court Grammar School

Warning: Hazardous

I walked into the chemical storage room; I looked cautiously around. *My God*, I thought, *there must be enough dangerous substances here to kill a person!* Suddenly I heard footsteps! She was returning then she appeared. She glared at me angrily. 'What are you doing in my make-up box?'

Alex Short (14)
Barton Court Grammar School

Blood

Drip, was the sound that woke me on that fatal night. And then again *drip*, I slowly opened one eye to see that the noise was coming from my brother's bloodstained mattress. I shut my eyes, then opened them again, but this was real; not a dream this time.

Alexander Montgomery (12)

Barton Court Grammar School

Entering The Sleep Of Death

My ears were ringing, pressure burning on my face.
My eyes had gone blurry and I couldn't feel my toes.
People in masks surrounded me with sharp objects.
I was at almost certain death and as my eyes closed
for the last time, I heard, 'We have injected the
anaesthetic.'

Sydney Henderson (11)
Barton Court Grammar School

Puppy Love

I walked in the door, then I saw her. Her deep brown eyes enchanted me, her hair smooth as silk. She was amazingly petite and from the way she looked at me I knew she was the one. I walked to the counter and said, 'That dog's perfect for me.'

Sam West (12)
Barton Court Grammar School

31

Dying In Battle

Men littered the green landscape, stabbed and sliced, their lives cruelly ended. The thundering sound of swords clashing in the background and the screams from innocent, dying boys, echoed all the way to the sea. Silence drowned their groans. They all stood up and bowed. The Battle of Hastings re-enacted.

Laura Briggs (13)
Barton Court Grammar School

Knife And Flesh

I heard the sickening squelch as I turned the knife in the flesh. A thick, red liquid leaked from the skin of poor dead Tom. Slowly, carefully I removed the murderous knife and then, once more plunged it right into his heart.

'Mum, please can I have a tomato sandwich?'

Robert Wilcock (14)
Barton Court Grammar School

Playtime

The sun shining down on me, people walk all over me, balls being kicked at me. Kids stamping on me, boys spitting down on me, some people even pull my roots out. I don't mind though as … I am grass.

Emma Inglis (15)
Barton Court Grammar School

Running

The sweat was pouring from her. Her heart pounding. Running so fast that she could no longer control her breathing. She started to sense him approaching. Getting closer and closer.
'Love, do you want a cup of tea for after your work out?'

Megan King (15)
Barton Court Grammar School

35

Beetle

The beetle was moving away fast as the rain poured down onto its back. A little bit of light was shining in front for vision in the dull weather and was desperately trying to take shelter. *Ding, ding,* the Volkswagen Beetle was locked and parked.

Helen Bailey (15)
Barton Court Grammar School

Where?

I'm travelling, round the world. Amazing, fantastic.
Seeing new places, meeting new people. No worries,
I'm excited. I close my eyes, spin the model globe
and place my finger on it. I'm going to Australia.

Alice Underwood (15)
Barton Court Grammar School

The Hedgehog

Bang! Flashing lights whizzing past and I am moving all over the place causing loud thumps. A scent of roses comes over me and I am drifting, silently now, through a sea of concrete. My spikes have smeared across wastelands. I have been decimated in my home.

Matthew Briggs (15)
Barton Court Grammar School

Jealousy

Nobody ever takes any notice of me. All I get to talk to is the dog - he's not much fun. Just because she saw him on the TV. I'm now her second best - condemned to the corner. Damn you Land of Leather!

Christopher Clark (15)
Barton Court Grammar School

Unheard Of Neglect

I'm opened up daily, people look at my insides, I'm scratched and torn, often people rip things out of me, there are millions of us, but none of us speaks up, I'm waved in the air daily, as the man yells, 'Books for sale.'

Benjamin Haff (15)
Barton Court Grammar School

40

Unsinkable

The orchestra were playing, Rose and I had on our best clothes. We'd been dancing all night, yet it felt like a mere hour. I gazed into her eyes, I was near to uttering, 'I love you,' but then, the ship struck an iceberg.

Daniel Geering (14)
Barton Court Grammar School

Silver Speed

You could hear it far away. It was gaining speed, going faster and faster. It was now visible, gleaming in the sunlight, with a small yellow dot cocooned inside. The crowd get to its feet. Lewis Hamilton's McLaren appeared on the TV.

Ashley Hibben (15)
Barton Court Grammar School

Spinning Like A . . .

The blue and green patched ball spins across the light
air. It rotates and twirls, passing all the watching stars.
I stand up and run across the blades of grass towards
a sign. The sign says: *Welcome to Earth*.

Andrew Pearce (15)
Barton Court Grammar School

Friends Forever

Age 12. I had my friend over from school. We kicked a ball around outside, shared some sweets that we had bought from the shop, baked some fairy cakes, sat down for some dinner and then my mum said, 'Aren't you a bit too old for imaginary friends?'

Philippa Page (15)
Barton Court Grammar School

Suddenfy

The hot sun beating down on my back, whilst I bathe in the midday sun. The fresh breeze occasionally brushing the tips of the large green parasols when suddenly a shadow begins to fall around me, increasingly getting darker. *Squish!* There goes the next insect, victim to the shoe!

Hefen Mifes (15)
Barton Court Grammar School

45

The Prison

I was stuck in eternal darkness, constricted into a small dark place, constricted by a rubbery rope to my place of dwelling. I lay there week after week trapped by my ever shrinking home.
Finally, I saw a light after 52 long weeks, I was born!

James Morris (15)
Barton Court Grammar School

Everyone Can Be A Hero

The boat riding the waves. I knew that this was suicide. I have to do it for my queen. The ramp lowered and we all charged off the boat. I was blown apart. I was killed as soon as I stepped onto the beach. My thorax and abdomen were everywhere.

Daniel Parrett (15)
Barton Court Grammar School

Sub-Zero

It's freezing cold, numbing my thoughts. I can't take this it's too much. This is the end, it must be. As my breath turned to ice in front of me and I looked down, it felt like the end of the world. I pulled my coke out of the fridge.

Milo King (13)
Barton Court Grammar School

48

The Chase

I fled, the wind whistling through my hair. Flashing lights followed me as I continued along the black track. It was dark and cold, the air had become still and the distant humming sound surrounded me as I waited at the traffic lights in my new convertible sports car.

Rachel Symons (13)
Barton Court Grammar School

Boxing Match

Hook, jab, hook. I now know the meaning of 'float like a butterfly, sting like a bee'. Every punch felt like being hit by a ton of bricks. All I could do was take the punches. But then I saw Mum. I punched him as hard as I could. Winner!

Harry Taylor (12)
Barton Court Grammar School

50

Problems

I racked my brain, and wrestled with it. Beads of sweat formed on my face. The strain was immense and burning my energy like a candle burns its wax. Was I a failure? No, it came to me, the answer of my maths question was one!

Lauren Baker (13)
Barton Court Grammar School

Facing The Enemy

Its teeth were so sharp and I was nervous. It was going to hurt me again, I knew it! It was gradually getting closer, its teeth shimmering in the light. I knew it was time, I had to face it, I'd no choice. I had to use the nit comb!

Lucy Hudson (13)
Barton Court Grammar School

The Falling Depth

All was dark. I was falling. My heart was racing. All I could hear was the screams of each and every one of my friends. How could they do this? I was sure I would die. Suddenly I saw the light. Flying from the flume as my friends awaited me.

Keefy West (13)
Barton Court Grammar School

53

The Terror In The Forest

It ripped through the forest, tearing the trees, shredding roots, smashing vines. It jumped into a tree and swung, pulling down trees, crushing animals under its massive feet. Vines tore, trees fell. The forest was flashing past as it rushed around the forest canopy. It was a vastly overweight chimp.

Andrew White (13)
Barton Court Grammar School

Thinking

Ten minutes left. How was I going to do it? This task was impossible! I was out of breath, I racked my brain, I felt dizzy, two minutes left, help! One minute, no that's not it! Thirty seconds, and yes! My maths test made sense! Kind of!

Hannah Wilson (12)
Barton Court Grammar School

The Prisoner

Took the glue, sealed the creature's mouth shut. Cheek to cheek. Pushed it into the prison. With the others. The officer came to release them. Shoved them into a sack and tied it shut. A woman picked up the beast, stabbed its stitches with a knife and opened the letter.

Rebecca Marsh (13)
Barton Court Grammar School

The Black Shadow

I held my breath for as long as I could, my blood pounding. The dark shadow on the surface, bobbing closer, closer, but the pressure on my lungs was too great. I burst up out of the water. The rubber yellow duck on the surface of the bath drifted past.

Rosanna Manser (13)
Barton Court Grammar School

57

The Game

The sun was set. All was quiet. It was time. I ran and ran, over all terrain. It was tiring, I got out of breath, but I continued. At last I reached level five.

Effy Reeves (13)
Barton Court Grammar School

Saved By The Bell

The paper was in front of me, it was messing with my head. The clock was tick, ticking, I was scratching it with my pen but nothing happened, then I heard it ring, I was free, I didn't have to do it, I didn't have to write my mini saga.

Effen Peirson (13)

Barton Court Grammar School

59

The Vegetables

They surrounded me, their bulging eyes glowing bright red. Wiping the sweat beads from my forehead, I tried to control my pounding heart. No use, the sickness was eating away. There was no use … I had to do it. Feeling nauseous I ate the thing … the Brussels sprout.

Dionyves Martin
Barton Court Grammar School

The Strange Man

The strange man in the white van came slowly down the road. Children were skipping and playing games in their front gardens. The sun's rays beat down onto every child, so they lay on the ground breathless. This was the man's time to strike, he shouted to them, 'Ice cream.'

Amy Farrant (13)
Barton Court Grammar School

It

It was approaching quite fast, clicking its sharp teeth.
I could see its shadow on the wall, it was massive!
Approaching even faster now, I turned to face it.
My heart was beating unnaturally fast. It opened its
mouth and screamed at me then I fed my little kitten.

Annie Hewitt (13)
Barton Court Grammar School

Perception

Slowly, I entered the room. Loud noises were emanating from the corner. Clunking and whirring. Whining and stamping. I knew this was going to happen; I made it so when I was last here. A long moan followed, and the noises ceased. I grabbed the printed sheet and walked out.

Dominic Howgiff (15)
Barton Court Grammar School

Finger On The Trigger

The little girl stood, horrified against the wall: A gun pressed against her thumping head. The man put his finger on the shiny, metal trigger. He began to pull it back, as the girl gave a high terrified squeal …
'And cut! That's it for today, thank you,' the director called.

Nicola Tapsell (15)

Barton Court Grammar School

64

Phone Call

The phone rang. I had been waiting for this call my whole life, but I couldn't answer it. My hands were clammy and I was shaking all over. A hand reached past me and answered the phone. There was a pause - deal or no deal?

Lamorna Manning (15)
Barton Court Grammar School

65

Big Mac

Sweat beaded my forehead. The insistent beep of
the machinery reminded me of where I was, as the
viscous liquid trickled through a matrix of tubes
beside me. They said I'd pull through, right? I placed
the greasy bag on the counter.
'£2.20 please. Thank you for eating at McDonald's.

Esmé Greenan (15)
Barton Court Grammar School

66

Speed

Faster, faster, just as I fell everything went blurry, was I in Hell? The ground was getting closer, would it hurt? I thought I regretted this and then I felt a sudden jerk. My near-death experience, was quite a thrill.
Let's do it again, bungee-jumping is brill!

Ryan Hatton (15)
Barton Court Grammar School

Flash

Deep darkness filled the cabin. Silence filled my ears.
All I could make out was these multicoloured blobs
blurring my vision. Then it stopped. It was time for
me to get off the train.

Dannielle Butcher (15)

Barton Court Grammar School

Clapping?

I was travelling and suddenly people started clapping for me. *How odd,* I thought. Well as people started clapping they got closer and closer to me until …
splat!
Kid, 'Finally, that mosquito was really annoying me.'

George Wilse (14)
Barton Court Grammar School

Running

Running through the woods, I was being chased
by maniacs with guns. I leapt through the bushes,
thought I lost them, but then … I was hit, covered in
red paint!

Sam Jenkins (15)
Barton Court Grammar School

No Escape

As we got further I got more worried, strapped down, no escape. This was it, I was almost over the edge - down into a large amount of water. I was tied so tight that there was no escape, why did they do this? Why was I talked onto this ride?

Rebecca Palmer (15)
Barton Court Grammar School

71

Adrenaline

As I hid behind a low wall, I could hear feet rushing past, faster and faster. The sound of screams and sinister laughs rang through my ears. Then the bell sounded. Lunch was over.

Ben McLean (15)
Barton Court Grammar School

Genocides And their Creators

There was an ecstasy of fumbling, everyone darting and diving. The engulfing green haze crept through the air, perpetuated in time itself. Everyone gasping for their lives, choking on the eradicating fumes of the demonic gas. It had happened. The exterminator was standing along the lawn, killing the parasites.

Joel Owen (15)
Barton Court Grammar School

The Reform Of The Bully

Why me? Just because I have glasses and braces they pick on me! I grinned and bore it but then it got worse with every painful punch. I wasn't going to say anything, but my friend did. I was angry. The bully approached me, 'Sorry,' he whispered. I stood stunned …

Ashleigh Sharif (13)
Canterbury High School

The Dentist

It was the moment of truth. I sat on the chair, 'Open wide.' He looked at my teeth, 'We can fit today.' I was terrified. We went down, the metal lines locked onto my teeth. The glue felt rubbery, but it was over. 'Ouch.' My mouth was aching for days!

Katy Haff (13)
Canterbury High School

Wolf Riding

Once in time there was a wolf named Wolf Riding.
She had to take some cakes to Grandma Wolf. When
she was on her journey a girl appeared.
'Give me that,' she said and took the cakes and then
she dragged Wolf Riding aside and ate her all up.

Danielle Nash (13)
Canterbury High School

Descent Into Darkness

I was shaking all over. We slowly got dragged up to
the sky, jolting all the way. We got to the top up in
the clouds. The view was phenomenal. We hung,
staring down to the dark cave lying beneath. '1, 2, 3.'
We plunged down and Oblivion was over.

Chloe Davies-Janes (13)
Canterbury High School

The Sapphire

My heart was pounding. I was running, sprinting more like! A powerful mighty knight was chasing me. I held a sapphire that the knight desperately wanted. I had stolen it from the royal castle. I fell. He stood tall. Held a knife to my throat, and then the book closed!

Sami Robey (13)
Canterbury High School

Cinderella

How dare they make Cinders do chores. Cinders got invited to a ball. I gave her a carriage and clothes. She had a fabulous time. But she left her shoe! The prince found her and the shoe fitted. They lived happily ever after. My work here was done. *Ching! Ching!*

Louise Potts (13)
Canterbury High School

The Big Bang!

Zooming along, suddenly, *bang!* Smashed to pieces as we were lifted out of the damaged object made to be in an unfamiliar place. We don't deserve to be here. Laying in our rough beds. Smelling of burnt out fire. We were laid in a body moulded shape and left there.

Chloe Jackson (13)
Canterbury High School

The Roller Coaster

The wind lifted our cheeks, as we fell forwards like floppy, soft teddies. We felt like jelly, as the wild ride carried us higher and higher, so high we were touching the clouds as soft as candyfloss. Suddenly, we flew towards the ground, our stomachs churned and we stopped.

Toni Beeching (13)
Canterbury High School

The Bermuda Triangle

It was calm at sea, sun shining brightly and you could see for miles until I looked to the south, where there was a big cloud of hazy mist and my ship called 'The Ginger Biscuit' was in the mist. We were never seen again until we docked at home.

Jack Bennett (13)
Canterbury High School

Forbidden Love

My thoughts lost in his blue ocean eyes. Our love was enchanting yet forbidden. A moment I will treasure forever when we sat by the tinted aqua lagoon side by side, watching the sunset. That's before my heart broke in two. Clutching my hands he said our love's forbidden.

Jodie Wyfie (13)
Canterbury High School

Snow White And The Seven Skaters

When I say Snow White you will think of the happy story, but what happens if she found the seven skaters instead? She found them in the skating park. All I can say is they didn't help, she died. How was she to know the death ramp wasn't a slide.

Emily Forbister (13)
Canterbury High School

Untitled

Far away a beautiful maiden was sleeping, having a dream about Prince Charming rescuing her, but with a twist. Her prince had found a more beautiful maiden. This made her angry so she woke up, found the maiden and had her breathing through a tube. That is a true tale.

Jessica Blake-Bowell (13)
Canterbury High School

YoungWriters

Untitled

It was a cold blustery night on the loch, we hadn't caught any fish for hours. We were just about to call it a day when we saw it, the Loch Ness Monster. It had big yellow eyes and slimy skin and in a blink of an eye it vanished.

Jack White (13)
Canterbury High School

Big Bad Wolf

Howdy it's me the big bad wolf and I'm off to blow some little piggies' houses down. So I went to the first little piggy's house and I huffed and I puffed and I didn't blow his house down. Instead I blew myself away. I landed in Jamaica, coconut time.

Daren Whaffey (13)
Canterbury High School

Behind Closed Doors

I wake up every day wishing that I could be in Heaven with my mummy. Daddy always injures me. I ask him to stop but he won't, he padlocks me in my room. I can't move, my room is under the stairs, I feel like a bird trying to escape.

Johanna Wilton (12)
Canterbury High School

The Story About Lilly

Lilly was kidnapped from her house. 'Help,' Lilly said as she lay there screaming, only to find no one was going to come. She lay there in pain hoping for someone to come. She was scared and hungry. Not long after she died.

Demi Pay (13)
Canterbury High School

Wedding From Hell

'Hurry up! Get your dress on.'
'I'm coming, don't moan!'
'You look gorgeous.'
'I know.' The car's here.
'Oh my God! My dress is pink, I look like a cherry.'
'You look fine.' (Beep, beep).
'I'm sorry, I can't go through with it.'
I was left alone at the altar.

Jasmine Easton (12)
Canterbury High School

90

My Birthday Surprise

On the day of my birthday I ran down the stairs like a cheetah and tried to sniff out where my family put my presents, but there wasn't any, but why? I looked at the calendar and it said 27th July, my birthday is 27th August. That's why.

Sydney Kennedy-Sanigar (11)
Canterbury High School

Jody And The Cat

One day Jody went to the park across the road. Jody found a black and white cat. Jody took the cat back to the house. She asked her mum to keep the cat. Mum replied, 'Yes, but you must take responsibility.' Jody was very happy and called the cat Violet.

Jessica Trapmore (12)
Canterbury High School

The Wolf's Big Fart

The wolf did not like living next to the three little pigs. So he went over and said, 'I'll blow your house down.'

'No,' said the pigs.

He huffed and puffed and did a big fart but the house was still there, but where was the wolf?

Jack Walbyoff (12)
Canterbury High School

93

Drenched!

Water gushed over me, splashing my limbs and face with great force. I reached out for something to grip the handle and stop the deadly water flow. Aha, a towel! I cautiously wrapped my shaking hand around the handle. 'Twist'.
'Daniel.'
'Yes Mum.'
'Stop hogging the shower.'

Daniel Nugent (12)
Canterbury High School

Poor Prince Charming

Cinderella receives an invitation to go to Prince Charming's party, but she doesn't want to go. Her fairy godmother turns up again and says, 'Go, he is perfect,' and makes her a wonderful dress, shoes, hair and a mini.
Then Cinderella says, 'What's the point? He is ugly!'

Leah Smith (12)
Canterbury High School

Untitled

A top spy has been planning a burglary for four years.
He set a date to do the burglary.
Two weeks later, that day came. He drove to the
mansion, he opened the door, it was unlocked. He
went in, there was nothing. 'Damn.' His sidekick had
got there first.

Alex Huckle (12)
Canterbury High School

Sleeping Beauty

Once upon a time Prince Charming was fighting through the bushes and trees to find the love of his life. He saw the tower, he walked up all 320 steps. He gave Sleeping Beauty a kiss, she woke up. He asked her to marry him but she walked off.

Tyler Coffard (12)
Canterbury High School

Little Blue Riding Hood

Once upon a time, Little Blue Riding Hood went to
deliver a cake to her brother, who lived in the wood.
She went off on her Mini Moto. On her way she saw
a big scary monster who ate her in one bite.

Offie Morhen (12)
Canterbury High School

The Fall

I'm worried wondering what will happen. I'm strapped to something heavy and I can't move. I'm getting to the top and then fall, waving side to side like a rag doll. I'm flying, I'm soaring, but I'm falling when suddenly *whoosh*, my parachute flies up, I fall lightly to the ground.

Lisa Crews (12)
Canterbury High School

3 Point Line

It's Jamie on the ball in this basketball final with the
score tied at 32-32 with 4 seconds left. Jamie shoots
from the 3-point line, it's going in! It goes blank.
Damn! That's the third power cut this week!

Nathan Browne (12)
Canterbury High School

The Last Stand

Down in York everyone is helping each other to
survive a terrible death.
One day everyone was suffering apart from one man
who can help them all.
The next day everyone got to work preparing food,
making shelters and getting to know each other.
During the night everyone died painfully.

Graham Hunt (12)
Canterbury High School

Stuck In Her Belly For Too Long

She's sitting there screaming. 'Why won't it come
out? It's been there for ages!' Her legs are wide
open, trying to push.
'Please help!' she screams to her husband.
'It's stuck,' he replies.
Then suddenly *pop!* She has let it out. That long
awaited disgusting *fart*.

Kirsti Santer (12)
Canterbury High School

102

Kidnapped

She opens her eyes to see a dark empty room. She
closes them again because she thinks it's a dream. As
she opens her eyes she screams for help.
Then she hears a voice, 'Shut up.'
She must have been kidnapped.
What happens next? You'll have to wait and see.

Demi Amos (11)
Canterbury High School

103

'Why Me?'

He whizzed around the country lane, wanting to tell his wife about his promotion at the hospital. Laughing to himself a sense of pride filled the air. Out of thin air, a lorry smashed into him, crushing his legs, his murmured cries were faint in the screeching fire.
'Why me?'

Katie Moss (12)
Canterbury High School

Snow White And The Baby Dwarf

'I'll see the dwarfs today.' Gets to the cottage, 'What a mess.' Tidies up. 'They'll be hungry, I'll make dinner.' Makes dinner. 'They'll be back soon.' Waits. 'When will they get back?' Baby comes in, 'Hi Baby where are they?' Baby says, 'They've packed their pickaxes and joined Shrek.'

Louisa Taylor (11)
Canterbury High School

Untitled

She slowly opened the creaky door, her heart thumping like a child on a trampoline. She peered around the corner and then she saw it, the chocolate cake. She tiptoed over to the table and gobbled all the cake up, yummy! Then a monkey arrested her for criminal damage!

Zoe Fryday (12)
Canterbury High School

The Silver Lock And The Key

Once upon a time in a bungalow in a daring woods.
Which had a big painted sign saying *No Entry*.
But one day a boy went in and found a tree with one
silver lock on the floor and a set of keys. He opened
the box and inside was £2,000. Wow!

Robert Irons (12)
Canterbury High School

This Amazing Car

'This amazing car has great acceleration with a top speed of 212 mph, with 6 gears. Around a sharp bend you will experience spectacular grip and with fantastic, new technology, off road, you won't feel a single bump,' he said.
Then the batteries ran out on the remote control.

Jamie Crouch (12)
Canterbury High School

108

Skoda

'So what's this car like?' said Jo.
'The new Skoda is great. It comes in silver, black,
blue and red. Inside it has electric windows, easy
changing gears, a leather steering wheel and free
cover for the seats.'
'How big is it?' said Jo
'About 17cm long and 13 cm wide!'

Kayley Oliver (12)
Canterbury High School

The Runaway Child

Sunday! I hated getting up at 7 just to go to a church!
Mum slammed the door. 'What do you think you're
playing at?' she shouted. 'Music … in church how
dare you?' she spluttered and with a sharp slap across
my face I flew out the door … I'd run away!

Lauren Blindell (12)
Canterbury High School

110

The Crazy Man From Down The Lane

There once was a crazy person who got his hands on a gun. He found a man walking down an alleyway and brought his gun out and shouted, 'I'm going to discombobulate you.'
The man replied, 'That doesn't make sense.'
He shouted, 'So?' and shot the man in the head.

Philip Knight-Stevenson (14)
Gravesend Grammar School for Boys

The House On The Hill

Thunder. Lightning. The house on the hill, the only source of shelter, it was here Charlotte ran, to get out of the rain. Once she was in, the door slammed. The stairs creaked - someone was coming towards her. She trembled, paralysed with fear, the door to her right creaked open.

Darren Horner (15)
Gravesend Grammar School for Boys

Dash (-)

After careful scrutinised thought my mini saga still did not have a title, therefore after the lesson it was supposed to be handed in. I received an after school detention for blatantly forgetting to do my homework, therefore my effort went down with my grades. I did not enjoy it.

Robb Henderson (15)
Gravesend Grammar School for Boys

The End Of An Era

Once upon a time there was a little man called Mike.
He had long hair on his head.
One day, he went to town, went into the library,
right to the top floor. He knelt by the window. He
opened his briefcase, took out his gun and fired at
Blair.

Kyle Ludlow (15)
Gravesend Grammar School for Boys

Once Upon A Time

Once upon a time there was a princess imprisoned in a tower, guarded by the Loch Ness Monster. A prince went to rescue her, when he arrived he saw her in the window.
'I'll save you,' he said.
Suddenly the huge monster appeared and the prince ran away, screaming loudly.

Matthew Blakemore (15)
Gravesend Grammar School for Boys

Alone Together

Cowering in the corner. The comfy room. 'They all
hate us,' he said
'No they don't,' I replied.
In my head I know they despise us. It matters not,
we are safe here, but must still hide in the recess.
Cowering in the corner, in the padded cell. Alone.

James Simmons (15)
Gravesend Grammar School for Boys

Rejected

Confident, we're picking teams. Everyone goes,
one by one. Just me left, rejected. Now we start.
A miracle! I'm given the ball. Now is my chance
to shine. I steam down the wing, I'm brilliant! But
everyone's laughing …
'Look at him move … backward Baywatch run, he's
off the pitch.'
Embarrassment.

Manbir Mand (15)
Gravesend Grammar School for Boys

Ran

He ran. No one knew where to or what from. Nine
o'clock like clockwork, we'd all be watching. Months
ago he disappeared.
'Maybe he's been caught,' 'Maybe he got there,' they
would joke.
Did he come or had he gone?
He came back late. Blood trailed. He ran, he fell.

Sam Mattacott (15)
Gravesend Grammar School for Boys

McDonald's Man

Alone in McDonald's, 'This seat taken?' he asked.
'No.' Sitting down he looked at my food, 'What?'
'Hungry.'
'Well this is my food,'
'Aaw …'
'I have some you can eat at home if you want.'
'Great.'
We went to my house that night. I got eaten by the
fat man.

James Griffin (15)
Gravesend Grammar School for Boys

119

Snake Charmer

Inches from death, inches from glory. I had followed it for hours; the serpent, through the deadly desert. I wanted to capture it, it would be mine. My hand extended. It turned, whispering, 'You can't have it all.'
It struck, and my pulse slowed. Wise serpent, it knew me well.

Brendan Johnson (15)
Gravesend Grammar School for Boys

Password

'*Argh!*' he's screaming again.
Just give it up. I don't have long. Whack.
'*Argh!*'
Still nothing. This one's going to tell me nothing,
maybe one of the others will tell me. Well, better
finish up here. Whack.
'*Argh!*'
This is your last chance, just tell me what the
password is!'

Thomas Saunders (15)
Gravesend Grammar School for Boys

It's Evil

The lightning twisted and flashed in the sky like some glowing snake. The bats flew overhead as the sun set. The evil professor laughed and screamed, 'I've done it.'
He had created the most evil and disgusting person ever to have walked the Earth. His name, well it's George Bush.

Sean Walsh (15)
Gravesend Grammar School for Boys

Class 10C

Stink bombs flying, here, there, everywhere.
People hiding under desks, hooligans laughing. The
teacher, not their usual teacher, unable to control
her students, e-mailing staff for assistance. Students
ignoring the teacher's commands, textbooks
everywhere, tables tipped over and chairs upside
down.
'10C! Calm down!' she exclaims, 'I hate kids!'

Ricky Dhami (14)
Gravesend Grammar School for Boys

No Way Out!

Over the darkening forest I fly. My feathers ruffling in the night breeze, my eyes set and ears pricked. I dive, I miss the prey. How do I get out? I fly up, but the trees keep me in. I hear an eagle, talons round my neck, saved by … Mummy.

Hannah Armitage (12)
Highworth Grammar School for Girls

TV Ends The World (With The Help Of The Dream Machines)

The day the world ended, people from every country imaginable, from Korea to Cuba, were sleeping soundly, blissfully unaware, dream machines switched on at full gusto. It fed people dreams, jokes and 3D telly from a satellite way up in space. That was what went wrong.
'Mayday! Mayday! Satellite overloading!'

Joanna Drury (12)
Highworth Grammar School for Girls

The Perfect Holiday

On a beautiful midsummer morning, I read peacefully in the garden, absorbing the sun's golden rays. The willow tree's slender fingers tickled my toes, and the flowers gazed up at me with innocent eyes. It was the holiday sent from God. I felt like the luckiest girl in the world.

Beatrice Casver (12)
Highworth Grammar School for Girls

Footsteps

The night was quiet and still, the moon shimmering and the stars twinkling. I lay on my bed staring out of my window. Strangely, I heard footsteps. Seconds later there was a knock on my door. The door creaked as it opened. A ghostly figure emerged from the darkness.

Sophie Elvin (12)
Highworth Grammar School for Girls

Stars

It was a beautiful summer's midnight. I lay, absorbed in the beauty of the glistening stars. I tried to create pictures within the stars, but all I could think about was Mum. I missed her, lying on that hospital bed 24/7. I looked up, her face smiling amongst the stars.

Hannah Forrow (11)
Highworth Grammar School for Girls

Waiting

She glances anxiously at the people around her, sweat pours off her face. She has been waiting six months for this day, it has finally arrived. She has practised many times, even planned her route. She is comfortable, she is ready, the doors open, the Next sale has begun.

Charley-Ann Waters (12)
Highworth Grammar School for Girls

129

In The Sky

In the sky, a girl with wings soars through the endless blue, free. She glides gracefully through the clouds. High up in the sky, the wind lifting her up into the light. She spreads her wings out wide, escaping her sadness and seeking for joy, fighting against her tragic fate.

Jenny Chen (12)
Highworth Grammar School for Girls

Terrified

My parents were out. I was all alone in my big dark house. There was a knock at the door, the handle creaked and the door slowly began to open. A big figure emerged, I hid in terror. I waited, the door slammed behind. I was surrounded by nothing.

Francesca Knope (12)
Highworth Grammar School for Girls

Smoking

A dark dreary night and I was walking through a creepy cemetery on my way home. I heard someone slithering up behind me but when I turned around … nothing. Black, misty, scary nothing. I trotted home. I wasn't scared.

Charlotte Tidd (12)
Highworth Grammar School for Girls

A Sunday In Summer

Clear blue skies all around. Trickling of a river passing by. Birds singing from leafy green treetops, whilst the sound of the ice cream van can be heard in the distance. Children playing happily in the grassy playing fields and the sound of buzzing bees can be heard all around.

Lauren Epps (12)
Highworth Grammar School for Girls

Lollipop!

John walked into Sugar Shack. He asked for a sugar free lolly. Suddenly the shopkeeper turned into a monster! 'Sugar free lolly!' he growled. The monster grew with anger! John went to run but the gruesome beast gobbled him up! John laid in its belly kicking and screaming. Scared.

Jessica Parrett (12)
Highworth Grammar School for Girls

134

Marriah

Marriah: Just a simple girl. Friends, boyfriend, A-grade student. An open-minded teenager that loves everything. Talked to everyone, liked everything. She loves her family, animals, pets, everything. A down to earth simple girl. Adventurous, loveable, amazing. She doesn't take, doesn't steal, honest, reliable, accepted by most. Bullied. But why?

Rachael Roberts (12)
Highworth Grammar School for Girls

Cats

Cats can be very strange creatures, some are cautious but many are pretty. They roam about at night, down damp alleyways doing nothing apart from stalking their own shadows, cast from the luminous moon above. But for many, they keep us company on lonely nights and are companions for life.

Eleanor Woolacott (12)
Highworth Grammar School for Girls

I've Got A Secret!

My mum said I've been like an imposter these past weeks. She also said I've been impudent! It's because I'm keeping something from her. It's my little secret! I'm frantic about it. It's fantastic! When she said, 'Why can't you tell me?' I was mutinous, I refused to tell her!

Giorgia Rowley (11)
Highworth Grammar School for Girls

Littering

It's something that is increasing rapidly and must stop. People always litter, and now, if you go to town or somewhere, all you will see on the ground is chewing gum and cigarettes. How many times do you see people dropping cigarettes or throwing them out of a car window?

Jenni Slade (11)
Highworth Grammar School for Girls

Attack

The sirens were going from both the police and the ambulance. The screams were coming from the panicking crowd. The streets were flooded, stained and smothered in the blood of innocent victims - some even children. One of them - the strange man with a black hood being led away forever …

Charlotte Curd (11)
Highworth Grammar School for Girls

139

My First Day

The door was twice my size. I looked back at my mum, she mouthed, 'Go in.' The brown door was menacing. I pulled the black, scratched knob. It squeaked. I stepped over the step and made my way down. I stepped over coats, books and bags. I turned and … 'Jack!'

Hannah Pape (12)
Highworth Grammar School for Girls

The Boy Who Screamed Too Much

Once there was a boy called Tom. He was extremely selfish and didn't care for anyone but himself. He gave his mother hell when they went shopping. If he couldn't have something he wanted, he would scream and shout childishly. But one day his head exploded from screaming too much.

Lucy Knowles (12)
Highworth Grammar School for Girls

Albatross

The albatross ruled the southern seas. Raising its chick in the safe tranquil wilderness. The peace was interrupted by merciless fishermen laying their long lines with hooks and bait. Thinking only of profit they lured this graceful bird to its death. Is it too late to save it from extinction?

Heather Connolly (11)
Highworth Grammar School for Girls

The Perfection Of Art

The perfection of drawing objects exactly how you
see it, with the shading just the right brightness.
Painting different shades of colour, making it look
as natural as you can. The feeling of finishing your
masterpiece, satisfactory accomplishment and proud,
makes all the hard work worth it in the end.

Rebecca Peat (12)
Highworth Grammar School for Girls

143

Ffower

It opens a tiny petal at a time; bigger it gets until comes into full bloom. Full of colour and life, representing all things good. But representing all the bad too, all the pain and suffering for the single flower represents every aspect of the world today.

Charlotte Cumming (12)
Highworth Grammar School for Girls

144

Lost

There I was, lying under the green oak tree. Lost.
Suddenly. I heard a high-pitched squeal echoing in the
dull, dark atmosphere. A blinding light shone from
the dark blue sky, shadowing the emptiness. I was
lonely, lost, scared, but there was nothing I could do
about it.

Jordan Stevens (12)
Highworth Grammar School for Girls

The Stalker

Turning round, a feeble man followed my footsteps.
From the corner of my eye I saw him speeding up.
It was quite strange … that an old man was able to
move at that speed. Seconds later, he pounced on
me like a jaguar … and I fell to the stony surface …

Monica Amorim (12)
Highworth Grammar School for Girls

The Crash

I couldn't breathe, ear-piercing screams filled the airtight plane. I grasped the seat with my sweaty palms as blistering flames climbed the aisle. My gut churned. The aircraft tumbled towards the icy ocean. I looked around to find nothing … no one. Just wreckage of a painful memory.

Courtney Pruce (12)
Highworth Grammar School for Girls

Terror Tide

Terrifying screams, tremble of fear, shaking shacks, glass cracking behind me, a huge wave hurling over my head. Running away tripping over my own feet, scared to death. I feel my shoes absorbing the gushing white water falling from the wave. Drips dripping on my head. Is it over?

Pippa Barnes (12)
Highworth Grammar School for Girls

The Monster Under My Bed

I sat in my bed, dead straight, the covers drawn up around me. I knew I shouldn't be up so late but I was too terrified to sleep. It wasn't my imagination; if it was, how did my dad just vanish in front of me? How do you explain that?

Kirsty Springett (12)
Highworth Grammar School for Girls

Stranded

They ploughed through the dense knot of branches in the jungle. The emerald foliage was an impenetrable wall around them. The wary travellers were lost for direction in the endless tunnel of leaves. The heat was unbearable. The travellers sat on a log but the insects soon scared them off!

Madelynne Wheaton (12)
Highworth Grammar School for Girls

Fluffy

One day a man went for a walk with his dog called
Fluffy. They were walking along a road, when a car
came past beeping its horn. The horn scared Fluffy
and Fluffy ran away. The man cried as he stumbled
home. He saw this fluff, it was little Fluffy.

Carla Reene (12)
Highworth Grammar School for Girls

The Wrong Train!

Me, Emily and Domi woke up from a sleepover. We got washed and dressed and travelled to the Ashford train station and bought tickets and got onto the Folkestone train. Off we go! The train started going, suddenly Emily knew the train split and now we are all doomed!

Megan Afecks (12)
Highworth Grammar School for Girls

152

Fly, Ohh Fly, The Life Of A Fly

A black dot. No one will see me buzzing around.
What's that? A bouncing bunny and a frightful fox.
Darting across the moors, between bramble bushes.
The gap's closing, the fox pounds on, the rabbit's
slowing and it pounces. I fly away. Oh no there's a
Venus flytrap … *snap!*

Natalie Elliott (12)
Highworth Grammar School for Girls

The Death Pool

I lie there in the sizzling heat. The temperature is boiling. I get in the pool; but the deep end by mistake. *Crash!* I can see the whole pool, then I realise. No beauty, calmness or life. I'm drowning. My death is approaching quickly. Blackness, Hell everywhere. I need help!

Moffy Miseham-Chappell (12)
Highworth Grammar School for Girls

154

Dance

I'm very shy. My friends are: Kim, Laura and Louise. Kim is the most confident. One day Kim signed me up for a dance competition. I was so angry. I spent three days preparing a dance. On the day of the dance competition, I won. I couldn't thank Kim enough.

Jessica Hardy (12)
Highworth Grammar School for Girls

The Cub

The cub was born under the starry sky, to the brightness of Earth, to be led by wisdom and courage. But one day, after a feverish hunt, the dogs came calling, barking and howling, with Man at their sides, and so the pack ran, and left the cub for dead.

Moffy Holt (12)

Highworth Grammar School for Girls

The Struggle For Life!

The struggle for life is long and hard. As soon as we are born we all have to fight. Fight for life, love and friendship. We grow but we still fight, we fight with and against family and friends, but we don't have to fight! But we still fight on. Life?

Rachel Drummond (12)
Highworth Grammar School for Girls

Another Bad Dream

I close my eyes dreaming a million dreams. Suddenly
I start falling through the air, twisting and turning
out of control. I can see vague outlines. I plummet
through the whipping wind. Then, a loud thud. I sit
up feeling dizzy. Scared. But, just another bad dream.

Sophie Marston (12)
Highworth Grammar School for Girls

The Hallowe'en Night

It was dark and cold that Hallowe'en. That night I walked through the alley. I slowly walked, feeling frightened till I froze from the breathing on my neck. I turned around and saw a luminous figure. Now I am writing this from my grave, ready to wander that alley again.

Ann-Marie Haycox (12)
Highworth Grammar School for Girls

Time

The clock struck twelve, midnight. The house silently slept on. Doors screeched on their hinges, and the wind howled outside. At the bottom of the garden, in the old potting shed, a small creature woke with a start. For, back in the house, in the lounge, the clock struck thirteen.

Elizabeth Bate (12)
Highworth Grammar School for Girls

Little Tanned White

Years ago, Little Tanned White stayed under her sunbed for so long she was burnt black. She remained under the sunbed for years until the eight dwarfs carried her to the forest and was placed under a new tanning bed. Little Tanned White is still waiting for the perfect tan.

Hannah Lumsden (12)
Highworth Grammar School for Girls

My Doggy

There once lived a girl named Molly who had a very cute doggy called Polly. They'd go to the park and her doggy Polly would bark. But one day Molly lost Polly! Molly was extremely upset but was hungry so bought a juicy lolly. She found her! Under her brolly!

Jodi Page (12)
Highworth Grammar School for Girls

Robbery

I was home alone. I began to drift off when the door opened. I thought it was Mum. I was wrong. I was being burgled! Shocked I dived under my bed and rang my dad, he called the police. They took the burglar. Now they never leave me home alone.

Emese Blenkinsop (12)
Highworth Grammar School for Girls

163

Drowning

My ribcage was being crushed under a wave of water. The breath squeezed from my lungs. Nobody here to listen to my calls, to pull me out, to rescue me. Pushing myself to my very limits, unable to take the strain. Drowning, drifting, floating to a watery grave. The end?

Victoria Baines (12)
Highworth Grammar School for Girls

Edge Of The World

I floated furiously towards a pool of blackness. An everlasting blackness. Wind whipping my sails. Water slapping my boat. I'm getting closer … and closer. Falling colours flashing all around me. Speeding towards the ground at immense speed. *Thud!* I'm in bed. Covers are on the floor and I'm cold.

Erin Samuels (12)
Highworth Grammar School for Girls

The Deep Freeze

Jamie and I stood here, frozen. Not sure how we got here; but we didn't care. We were together. The sun sunk with our hearts. We died on our wedding night. My eyes shine when I remember that when our hopes had left us, we did not desert each other.

Jennifer Baker (12)
Highworth Grammar School for Girls

The Haunted House

Stacey and Beky ran from the house, But Beky tripped and Stacey was nowhere to be seen. Beky tried to run, but she saw a figure in the background. She decided to stay put, but then out of nowhere, Stacey grabbed her friend's hand and they ran away.

Melissa Murphy (12)
Highworth Grammar School for Girls

The Ugly Kitten

Once there was a family of kittens, all white except for one. He was brown and black. The family rejected him so he went to the street. He found a new, caring family. They were all different fat, thin, young, old and the kitten never, ever felt left out again.

Katharine Sheppard (12)
Highworth Grammar School for Girls

Untitled

My heart was pounding, I couldn't breathe, I was scared for my life! Scrambling down the hallway I tripped and he grabbed my leg! After being dragged down the stairs, he stopped. He stood still, just watching, watching the door. A tall figure emerged. Who was it? Then pitch-black.

Jasmine Bailey (12)
Highworth Grammar School for Girls

Friday 13th

18.00. Hi I'm Lucinda and today has been the worst day of my life. I'm 14 today and I woke up to find Holly had weed on my bed, Dad fell in my cake and well, I'll give you some advice. Don't go out on Friday 13th!

Larren Jeffries (11)
Highworth Grammar School for Girls

The Bully

I thought it was cool to bully the smart kid in school.
Whenever she was right I mocked her. Then she
didn't come to school because she was being bullied.
She stayed at home as she couldn't take anymore.
We asked the teacher what we could do to help her.

Emma Dean (12)
Highworth Grammar School for Girls

171

Secret

There is a story of a secret story, but I can't tell you the story of a secret story because, if I tell you the story of a secret story you might tell someone else the story of a secret story, and it wouldn't be a secret anymore, would it?

Rachael Hooper (12)
Highworth Grammar School for Girls

Dead

A woman was thrown out onto the street. She was down but soon got back up and walked home. Her bag was snatched. She picked up a brick and threw it. She looked down, disgusted, dropped her bag and ran for miles, to the cliffs. She didn't stop running.
Splash!

Lucy Bird (12)
Highworth Grammar School for Girls

173

Rubber Band

There is a rubber band called I and one called You.
They live in a rubber band world. I bought a guitar
and You bought drums. They're in a band called
Rubber, so they really are a rubber band! (I'm their
number one fan!)

Kate Richardson (12)
Highworth Grammar School for Girls

174

Say No

She says they convinced her to take it, trying to fit in with everyone else. I've learnt from her mistakes, I'll never smoke. It's not good for your health. Smoking kills and it makes you smell. It harms others around you. I don't care what they say, I'll tell them.

Georgina Heisley (11)
Highworth Grammar School for Girls

When I Tried To Fly

When I was a little girl, I tried and tried to fly. But whenever I tried I always seemed to hurt myself and I always wondered why. My mother said, 'Oh why, oh why must you try to fly, you could hurt yourself and maybe even die. Oh why?'

Sophie Smith (11)
Highworth Grammar School for Girls

Perdie The Parrot

Every morning Perdie the parrot would wake up, get out of his nest and squawk loudly. Perdie enjoyed doing this but the man across the street was not very happy with Perdie, so the man came out of his house and *bang!* Perdie was nowhere to be seen!

Emily Rogers (12)
Highworth Grammar School for Girls

Little Bo Jeep

You've all heard of Bo Peep, haven't you? But what happens in the end? Her sheep attracts a farmer. Bo Peep and the farmer fall in love. The farmer finds he is allergic to sheep. In the end they sell the sheep, buy a jeep. Now she's Little Bo Jeep!

Amy O'Donoghue (12)
Highworth Grammar School for Girls

Scrooge

Scrooge was the nicest man ever. One night Scrooge was haunted by his ancestors, they were horrible. All night they were trying to make him bad. Scrooge saw the benefits of causing grief. From then on Scrooge became very rich. He soon became Prime Minister, I wonder why?

Stephanie McCourt (12)
Highworth Grammar School for Girls

What To Do Now

Lola woke up. *Another day of protest,* she thought.
She and her best friend went to the Brooke animal
testing protest, every Saturday since they were
twelve. Though today was the last protest. After the
years of fighting they had won. But what would they
do now with their lives?

Amber Good (12)

Highworth Grammar School for Girls

Silly Dreams

One day I tried to fly! It didn't work! My mum rushed
as she heard a bang and said, 'Why did you try to fly?'
I cried, 'I wish I was a bird soaring above in the sky,
drifting upon the pockets of air, freedom.'
My mum cried, 'Silly dreams!'

Jemma Taylor (11)
Highworth Grammar School for Girls

181

Under The Purple Tree

Under the purple tree lived goblins who ate everything that touched the tree. One day Ellie let go of her balloon and it stuck to the purple tree. The goblins dashed up the tree. When they touched the balloon it popped. They never ate anything on the tree, ever again.

Olivia Ruddock (12)
Highworth Grammar School for Girls

The Butter Bread Man

Every day when the Butter Bread Man walked down the road, he was pecked at by birds. One day he was granted the power to transform into a scarecrow to chase birds away, whenever he liked. Now birds don't peck at him in case he turns into the scarecrow again.

Danielle Tomlinson (12)
Highworth Grammar School for Girls

Slash

Alone. Creaking, cracking doors slamming in the haunted house. She was finding her way through the dark and damp depths of the corridor. Her pace slowly increased, her heart rapidly beating, telling her to take just one look behind her.
Face; saggy, old.
Slash! She was never seen again.

Eleanor Cleasby (12)
Highworth Grammar School for Girls

184

Untitled

My best friend, one minute here, next minute gone. Nobody knows the touch of the frosty, icy fingers laying on your shoulder and bang you're gone. The worst part is you can't see it come and get you. I will find out. Our small village of Smarden, not many suspects.

Hannah Coutts (12)
Highworth Grammar School for Girls

True Love Comes In Different Ways

Georgina ran. She gained her speed as the shadow behind her moved closer. She could feel it coming closer to her. Frightened, she turned around. It was William.
'William! What are you doing here?' she yelled. William didn't say a word, he bent his head and kissed her.

Jacqueline Perry (12)
Highworth Grammar School for Girls

186

Fireball

I was travelling fast, bending. I was on the Rock 'n'
Roller roller coaster when suddenly we stopped, a
sudden halt. I panicked. Afterwards, slowly the roof
started opening, it was getting hotter, then we saw
it, the great fireball! It came closer and now we are
stuck forever!

Stephanie Owen (12)
Highworth Grammar School for Girls

Lost

The ship was swaying steadily in the musky, gentle breeze. Some say it was haunted, some just say it's a myth. The crew were all set and ready for the long, sticky journey back to the port.

'Where was John,' the crew asked themselves?

A wailing, a screaming, a shouting, lost forever!

Chloe Garner (12)
Highworth Grammar School for Girls

Alone In The Woods

'What was that?' I asked myself, as I rushed over twigs and branches in the creepy, dark woods of Pluckley. I was terrified as I heard noises behind me, closer and closer. I started running faster. I looked around, but there was nothing there. Was it my father's ghost?

Sarah Adrian (12)
Highworth Grammar School for Girls

The Dream

I woke up, sweating. The dream seemed so realistic!
Rushing to the window, I looked down. My worst
nightmare had come true! Star had gone! Star, the
only creature I trusted, gone. I fled downstairs into
his paddock and cried. Coming back to my senses, I
ran.

Effie Keenan (12)
Highworth Grammar School for Girls

Mystery

As the black of the night swirled through the trees,
footprints appeared on the ground before me, I
stopped. Unaware of what was there. Unsure of the
way to go. I shivered, something moved beyond me.
My heart racing at full speed. Then there it was, the
darkest nightmare ever.

Zoë Parton (12)
Highworth Grammar School for Girls

Disaster

I was running, running through the forest, running away from everything. I got lost, then something came behind me. I turned around, I couldn't see anything. I was pushed, pushed off the cliff, pushed to my death. I woke up, it was just a nightmare!

Emily Horton (12)
Highworth Grammar School for Girls

Scream

Walking up the winding path to the creepy haunted house, my heart beating fast. The windows cracked, the wooden door broken. I tiptoed up the creaky steps. Suddenly the door flew open. A bony hand grabbed me, pulling me inside. I found myself standing in an endless hall of darkness …

Victoria MacMillan (12)
Highworth Grammar School for Girls

Internet Boy

He seemed nice. I thought he was my age. I didn't know. He hurt me and made me feel upset. I came home, told my mum. I still remember. Remember that day when my Internet boy turned out to be an old guy who hurt me.

Aimee Hyder (12)
Highworth Grammar School for Girls

The Huntsman's Dog

His muscles tensed. His whiskers twitching. Glaring at his prey. Their eyes met and for seconds there was silence. The dog growled, the rabbit bounding away at a moment's notice. It was too late, the rabbit was gone.

Alice Goldstein (12)
Highworth Grammar School for Girls

Danger Lurks

I watched as the small box erupted into millions of
fiery pieces. Then we got showered in dust. *Bang!*
The marquee was on fire. I was being surrounded by
thick black smoke.
'Help,' I yelled! Nobody could hear me, then a hand
grabbed me. Was I safe or not?

Georgina Benson (12)
Highworth Grammar School for Girls

A Dream - No

Earlier, our money was stolen. Then before our bonfire party, myself and Mum discovered a strange rocket. Dad came over, then the rocket went off. A voice, 'There goes your money and now us.' *Bang!* A bomb blew up, we were lying on the ground, dead!

Emma Chapman (12)
Highworth Grammar School for Girls

Mousetrap

He ran in screaming, 'They're coming.'
I turned, scared, from the window. Tom was
panicking, trying to find a way out.
'No they're not,' I suddenly realised, frantic. The den
was made of wood.
'Tom!' I cried.
Crackle, angry flames burst from nowhere. Scorching,
searing, pain.
'Mum, Dad,' then nothing.

Alissa Cooper (12)
Highworth Grammar School for Girls

Spell Hard

Harriet sneakily tiptoed into the room of requirement. Wands were at the ready. Technicolour sparkle filled the room with mighty pink sparks, Mr Docherty covered the door, then the words Avada Kavada, came firing from his mouth, aimed for Harriet. She froze, then Mildred jumped in front. Mildred was dead!

Christina Roberts (12)
Highworth Grammar School for Girls

My Stepdad

She screamed. *Bang!* he yelled, another bang. You could hear her breathing heavily. He yelled at her again. She cried in pain. I sat there and listened to her yelp in pain. Glass smashed, she didn't scream this time. My door handle turned. He stood in the doorway, I screamed …

Charlotte Denniss (12)
Highworth Grammar School for Girls

200

The Gun

The gun, to her confused head. The gun, to her confused children. The gun, to her community. What had they done wrong? Was it the colour of their skin? Was it their beliefs? The babies screaming, adults trying to keep calm. Then the dreaded noise, the village devastated.

Alice Metcalf (12)
Highworth Grammar School for Girls

What Does It Mean?

She looked into her crystal ball. I asked what she
could see. She replied, 'Nothing.' There was a long
silence, then Gemma yelled out that she could see
something, it was Jake and I. He was telling me
something. I burst into tears, what could this mean?
The future?

Lizzie Lukehurst (12)
Highworth Grammar School for Girls

The Statue

He walked, slowly, step by step through the pyramid. Would the statue appear? He knew it was with the mummies, but where were they? As he turned the corner, there they were … the mummies! The lid crashed open. He picked it up. Finally he had it. It was his!

Rebecca Bowes (11)
Highworth Grammar School for Girls

The Basement

That's it! We're fed up with our uncle telling us not to go in the basement. Well, it doesn't matter anyway because we're going in.

We came to the old eerie door. This is it! We went for the handle, opened the door, to find it there, in the dark …

Davina Lewandowska (12)
Highworth Grammar School for Girls

The Stranger

Late one night there was a strange noise. One person, riding a skeletal horse, heard it. He landed in a snowdrift, leaving no marks. There was a goat lying in a pool of blood.

'Come with me,' the robed stranger said.

'Oh, you're Death!'

Then the goat vanished.

Amy Gibbons (12)
Highworth Grammar School for Girls

Haunted

Hollow eyes bore into my mind, the ghastly spectre was staring. It was reading me like a book. I should have believed my friends, how would I know my house was haunted by the ghost of an old resident? I am trapped, no, cornered. Who knows what will happen now?

Catherine Troman (12)
Highworth Grammar School for Girls

Frogs

Frogs ... jump, leap, hop, spring, bounce, but this frog walks, talks and runs. Some frogs croak, but this one sings as it walks, talks and runs. Many frogs eat flies, but this one eats orange berries and cake, as it sings, walks talks and runs.
Well, that's Milo for you.

Charlotte Judge (12)
Highworth Grammar School for Girls

207

Snap

Sitting graciously on the riverbank, head bowed low,
waiting for the ideal opportunity. As he waited, he
sharpened his claws.
Next, he positioned his back legs ready to pounce.
He ground his teeth together as he spotted his prey.
As fast as lightning he bolted towards the helpless
fish! *Snap!*

Lucy Ibbetson (12)
Highworth Grammar School for Girls

208

Howl to The Moon

The attitude of the wolves on a balmy fall night, is strangely extraordinary. These savages assemble and howl to the light of the dark. When the moon is entire, they sing to the great spirit wolf. The wind cries, 'Go and hunt my children. Your blood is hot in excitement.'

Hannah Wooffey (12)
Highworth Grammar School for Girls

209

The Photo

Jenny stared at the old dusty photo. She looked, there stood a little girl; she looked sad, betrayed. Around her stood photos of Jenny's friends, their eyes full of terror. They had been stalked like prey and viciously murdered. Jenny's photo was there, she began to sweat. Was she next?

Shannon Galvin (12)
Highworth Grammar School for Girls

Vampost - The Beginning

Vampost is a named feared by all, for Vampost is a vampire ghost. He is so widely feared that he has no friends, but he doesn't care, for he enjoys scaring and hurting and killing. They caught him, trapped him, he escaped. Now he has disappeared - pronounced dead.

Alice Bessant (12)
Highworth Grammar School for Girls

The Silly Seal

Splashing on ice, swishing his tail, balancing a ball on the tip of his nose, whilst wildly hooting to attract others. He smoothly glides to the edge of the ice and dives into the refreshing ocean.
Suddenly, he screams with pain and collapses. A shark has killed the silly seal.

Sarita Kang (11)
Highworth Grammar School for Girls

No Way Out

I stood there. Blood seeping through my clothes. I needed to find a way of getting to the time machine, before that terrifying beast clapped eyes on me. I moved cautiously, begging not to stand on a twig; but I did. The creature's eyes turned, looked directly at me!

Heather Campbell (13)
Highworth Grammar School for Girls

Seeing Double

She had just met her brother, her brother who was dead. Yet in his world it was her that no longer lived. She no longer knew anything. Her life was like a box; the lid had just been opened. The light was pouring in and the mist had risen.

Catherine Pritchard (13)
Highworth Grammar School for Girls

Me, Mum And Dad

I stumbled across the long grass, feeling cool air brush onto my burning, tear-stained cheeks. The leaves of the bush next to me slid between my fingers. I didn't want to go home. I hated it there. My mum and dad shouting, only this time, over me.

Rachel Hills (13)
Highworth Grammar School for Girls

Last Hope, Gone

I shut my eyes closed. The darkness flooded through me. I shivered like an electric current ran through me. Voices whispering and quiet murmuring. I felt water drip slowly onto my head. Gasped. Opened my eyes, a luminous light pierced through them, drowning my face in tears. Coldness, numbness, nothing.

Lottie Gibbons (13)
Highworth Grammar School for Girls

Revenge

Lying on my bed in the darkened room. I tried to block it out, but the banging continued. 'Open up,' they ordered. I wouldn't come out. Not for anyone. They had already taken the only things I ever loved. Full of rage, I decided that it was time. For revenge.

Kate Barker (13)
Highworth Grammar School for Girls

First Day

It's Sophie's first day of school and she's very scared.
She gets out her car and steps through the door.
People there to greet her. Unfamiliar faces, yet
friendly. They take her away, around the school.
Makes some friends. With a big grin, she goes back
home in her car.

Sherri Morris (13)
Highworth Grammar School for Girls

The Beating Never Stops

Anna came home from school on Thursday and noticed something strange. She walked over to the computer and suddenly she felt a rhythm in the computer speakers, it was a heartbeat. Anna drew back in fear, and with that her own heartbeat had joined in with the mystery.

Marianne Edwards (13)
Highworth Grammar School for Girls

Fear

I stumbled over my feet, begging for forgiveness. He edged closer and closer, causing me to go further towards the edge of the cliff. Rocks broke off and drifted down thousands of feet below. I cowered behind my hands, overwhelmed with hatred. I clenched my fists, ready to fight back.

Lucy Gray (13)
Highworth Grammar School for Girls

Untitled

The breeze blew across the icy river. Roses covered in frost, glistening in the moonlight. Grass had been chilled and iced over, as cold as a dead, broken heart. Hear it crisp underneath you as you tread. The frozen river, silent, still. It was filled with hatred and sorrow.

Gemma Reynolds (13)
Highworth Grammar School for Girls

Dreaming

They all pointed, mouths opened, wondering how
this could have happened. Me, the school's swot,
linking arms with the coolest boy in the universe.
Heading for the hall doors, entering the prom. All
night we danced along to the music.
'Tracy, get up, you'll be late for school,' said Mum.

Harriet Pepfoe (13)
Highworth Grammar School for Girls

The Test

We all entered the hollow room. It was set out like a prison cell. We all gathered in the murky dungeon, sitting apart, waiting for it to be over. The sullen silence made my nerves increase. The gun fired.
Bang! Bang! Bang!
The test had started.

Alice Bartholomew (12)
Highworth Grammar School for Girls

Escape Plan Number 7

'Dig boys,' the duck ordered. They were going to escape from the farm. He saw a monkey. 'Where are we?' he asked.

'Hawaii,' it said with an Hawaiian accent!

'Far too hot for us, come on boys, we're going home!'

That was escape plan number seven down the pan.

Bethan Cole (12)
Highworth Grammar School for Girls

A Mysterious Mystery

A body, a suspect, a crime. A suspect, but not a suspect anymore, another victim instead. So now who's the suspect? Two murders, no suspect, two crimes. The search starts, the clues link, but who's to blame? Nobody knows who's the murderer, except the murderer themselves!

Abbie Ward (12)
Highworth Grammar School for Girls

Don't Travel Fast

It was Saturday morning, we were all preparing to go on our holiday. We got our suitcases and packed them into the car. We were so excited and were all singing on the journey. But on the motorway we were driving fast, before we knew it, darkness appeared.

Eve Hickmott (12)
Highworth Grammar School for Girls

226

Kidnap

I was lying alone in my bed. I couldn't sleep. I twisted, I turned. Closing my eyes I lay down. Mixed memories filled my mind. Suddenly, there was a *bang!* My door swung open, a black figure approached me. I screamed for help! No one came. I was gone forever!

Isabella Derosa (12)
Highworth Grammar School for Girls

The Case Of The Missing Underwear

Well this is confusing, where do I start? My underwear's missing. I know I'm the detective but someone has stolen my underwear from right under my nose. I shall investigate.

First I shall interview my family. Actually, no, I'll start by searching the house.

Oops! … I remember, I'm wearing them.

Jennie Mackay (12)
Highworth Grammar School for Girls

Cinderella

Cinderella was sweeping up ashes. Surprise! A man knocked on the door. 'An invitation to the Tramp's Ball!'

When Cinderella arrived at the ball, she danced with the tramp all night.

When Cinderella got home the tramp said, 'Will you marry me?'

She snorted, 'No way, you absolutely stink!'

Paige Davies-Helme (12)
Highworth Grammar School for Girls

Escape

Had I escaped or was he still there? Had I escaped
or could I still see that glare? Running, I tripped, I
couldn't see. I closed my eyes, how long was I there?
Long enough for him to find me. Will this nightmare
never end?

Yovayfa Aryee (12)
Highworth Grammar School for Girls

The Dream

I jumped, then I fell. I swirled, then I flew as high as the sky. Did anybody see me? I don't know. Then I saw something, a big, orange ball, floating in thin air, surrounded by what looked like white pillows. Then I woke up.

Lily Murphy (12)

Highworth Grammar School for Girls

Touch

It's glaring at me - I'm scared, frightened. There is a
shiver creeping down my spine and it won't go away.
The ghostly figure is reaching towards me. So afraid I
feel sick. Its pale hand is coming closer. As it touches
my face, I faint. Where am I?

Chloe Rainbird (12)
Highworth Grammar School for Girls

Moonlit Night

In the dark mist of the moonlit sky, I sat alone, as the stars blinked and shimmered in the sky above. I lay back, closing my eyes. The sound of nature rocked me to sleep. I found myself falling into my own world. I was dreaming, dreaming the night away.

Yasmin Friend (12)
Highworth Grammar School for Girls

She's Coming To Get Me

She's chasing me. I don't know how long I can stand
it. I have got to go and tell them. They can help. But
what'd she say? Or rather what would she do? She
hates me. She punches me straight in the stomach.
'It's all your fault!' she says

Eleanor O'Doherty (12)
Highworth Grammar School for Girls

Murder Gone Wrong

Running through the woods, with nowhere to hide from the bloody murderer. She was gasping for an icy breath. Blood was on her hands, tears on her cheeks; she fainted with disgust and disbelief. Opening her eyes, she saw the figure of a woman, the woman in black!

Caroline Dewar (12)
Highworth Grammar School for Girls

Footsteps

I lay on my back, staring out of my window. I couldn't
sleep. I heard approaching footsteps, coming closer.
I opened my mouth to call out, but I was too scared.
Alone, I stood up, I edged forward, my breath in
short gasps. The door creaked open, I screamed!

Paige Craßß (12)
Highworth Grammar School for Girls

Bad Luck

Looking out of my bedroom window, a rush of panic shivered through me, as my friend's house was bombed.

Blinding orange and yellow flames burned up another family home. Surprisingly, I saw three figures running towards my house. *Good, they're safe,* I thought. Unexpectedly another bomb exploded in their path.

Melissa Grace (12)

Highworth Grammar School for Girls

The Feeling

Tina strolled along, the trees' leaves began to rustle
as if they were whispering to Mother Nature. The
clouds drew a dark, grim image and blackened the
sun as though they were trying to erase it.
The feeling poured over Tina; allowing her no time
to embrace it.

Grace McMuffon (12)
Highworth Grammar School for Girls

The Storm

The thundering noise came raging through the tall trees. The wind howled maliciously and the sky filled with dark, sinister shadows. The rain fell heavily, like hard merciless rocks. Trees shook, leaves crackled. It was dark and dismal. Then it was still, quiet but cold. The storm was finally over.

Effis Dean Odey (12)
Highworth Grammar School for Girls

239

The Old Factory

I was static with fear, I heard screeches echo through the dark halls. The lights flickered, a gust of wind whipped open the curtains. The most sinister moon shone, revealing my best friend, lying on the rat-ridden floor. Blood trickled from his nose, like a cold tap, *drip-drop!*

Ruby Norris (13)
Highworth Grammar School for Girls

Bluewater . . .

Shops open; rush in. smell of food, long queues.
Dorothy Perkins, new earrings. Lancôme, more
make-up. *Oh my God!* Famous star, Victoria Beckham,
autograph. Whoo, wicked!
Lunch time, eat food, drink and pay. More shops,
more bags. Get in car, drive off, onto the motorway.
Home at last!

Catherine Cooper (12)
Rainham School for Girls

Two Deaths In A Week

Woke up. silence. Crying - pale faced.
'What's happened?'
'Grandad's dead love.'
Sad, burst out crying. Went to bed. Woke up,
presents; Nan's birthday. Damn! Forgot!
Went to bed at 9pm. Woke up, phone rang, my
uncle. He was sad. Mum was crying. I overheard;
'Grandma's dead.'
Noooo!

Jenny Stephen (12)
Rainham School for Girls

242

Over The Horizon, Never To Be Seen Again

As he boarded, tears fell down my cheeks. There I stood, watching him as he mouthed, 'I love you.' Before I knew it, the boat had departed. I'm standing there shouting, 'Come back! Come back!' I can no longer hold in my tears, I can't live without him.

Jessica Hawkins (12)

Rainham School for Girls

The Guinness Pig

At home, I check my guinea pig. He's fine, very hyper. I look, the cage, water bottle; it has Guinness in it! No wonder he is hyper.
From that day we have called it a Guinness pig. How did it happen? I wonder.

Hayley Venus (12)
Rainham School for Girls

A Cinderella Story

Alone, washing the dirty floor.
'Cinderella, Cinderella, clean my room. Cinderella,
Cinderella, make my bed.'
Ding dong, rat-a tat-tat. 'Cinderella, answer that
stupid door!'
Answering the door, 'You're very beautiful, Princess,
will you marry me?'
Yes, luckily, finally, Cinderella is happy.

Hoffy Bufford (12)

Rainham School for Girls

The Dragon-Slayer

Daman, a fierce lion-eating dragon-slayer, who could kill anything.

One day, a dragon came swooping across the castle, breathing fire heavily. Daman shot and stabbed until the dragon was no longer alive.

He was the hero and managed to save everyone. He was a star - Daman the great.

Grace Klimkowicz (12)
Rainham School for Girls

Plane Trip

On the plane. Off somewhere nice. Next to my sister, annoying or what! Eating breakfast. *Minging!* Watching Peter Pan. Sister annoying me. punching, me. baby crying, Grandad snoring! Playing on PSP Battery gone. Sister asleep. Dinner quite nice. Off the plane, legs gone dead; Oh no! Pins and needles.

Amelia Scott (12)
Rainham School for Girls

Cinderella - The Break Up

Happy ending? Think again! Turns out not so charming! Not had wash since wedding. Smelly feet, stinky breath. Thinks he's Mr James Bond! Wants children, he should be so lucky! Wish I'd left him to the ugly sisters. Single's not so bad. Filing for divorce, couldn't stand him any longer!

Aimée Vaccarello (13)

Rainham School for Girls

The Disaster At 5 O'clock

It was 4:30pm. Coming home from school.
'What a day,' said Mum.
'Yeah, what else can happen,' Sam replied.
They drove on, went the countryside way. Dark!
Raining! Stormy! Mum sleepy, eyes drooping. *Skid!*
Bang! 5 o'clock, all dead.
What a day for Mum and Sam!

Rebecca Walkiden (12)
Rainham School for Girls

Missing Mummy Already

Just been taken in a black bag, don't know where I'm going, so scared. Shoved into a dark room. Missing Mummy already, want her back holding my hand. Mysterious man coming towards me. I'm scared. I scream.

'Where's my Mummy? I want you Mummy, I miss you very much.'

Anastasia Lusinski (11)
Rainham School for Girls

Dramatic End

'Showtime, props everyone!'
'I wouldn't talk to her, she's still angry with me. She can take it out on me in the finale. The sun will never rise again!'
'That's no way to think.'
'No I meant … for you!'
Stab. Applause.
'Call an ambulance! She's dead!'
'Police!'

Lauren Feekings (12)
Rainham School for Girls

The Peach

Its warm skin touches rosy red lips of the girl. She
licks her lips and swallows the last tasty mouthful.
Her stomach feels funny, she feels sick, her head
even hurts.
She falls to the ground and never gets up again. The
reason, true, she turned into a peach.

Julie Bowcock (12)
Rainham School for Girls

Who Am I?

Sat up … where? Small room - hospital! People
surrounding, confused scared.
'Sweetie, thank you God!' hugging.
Man: 'You OK … Carla what's wrong?'
Nurse: 'Give her some room.'
'Who? What?' heavy breathing.
'Dear, you've been in a coma for four years …'
'W … who are you w … who am I?'

Hannah Tapson-Rees (12)
Rainham School for Girls

253

What A Day

Coach journey; long. Traffic, more traffic. Finally in,
let's go, people scatter. Wow, that was fast! Steep,
flashing lights, darting here there and everywhere.
Up, down, side to side. Soaking wet, will I ever dry?
All sorts of rides. Quick! One more ride. Time to go.
Oh, more traffic!

Grace Robinson (12)
Rainham School for Girls

Albert The Egghead

Albert was loved by many girls, but the only thing he loved was boiled eggs! Before long Albert began to steal them. The wizard was around the next morning and said as he liked eggs so much, he would be one and so now he is a boiled egg!

Lyndsay Kreffe (12)
Rainham School for Girls

Instinct

Claws spread, eyes squinted, body tightly pushed together, watching … waiting … for the right moment to pounce. People passed by, not noticing the piercing eyes of the furry creature. The patient creature swished its tail in annoyance as the prey started to move. The cat pounced, grasping the poor innocent creature!

Bethan Horne (12)
Rainham School for Girls

256

Where Am I

The door screeched open, scraping the floor on its hinges, webs dangled high on the ceiling, scrunched up like candyfloss. Shadows with piercing eyes surrounded me in this deadly place. Dust situated on the black windowsill, a view of a misty deserted garden …
A strange, curious place, a haunted house!

Jasmine Claydon (11)
Rainham School for Girls

257

Mica Has No Friends

Mica had no friends, she was bullied and nobody seemed to care. But she had an imaginary friend called Charlie. Charlie went everywhere with her, the park, beach and school. But Charlie never said anything to her; nobody else could see Charlie except her. Mica realised that she was lonely.

Broch Anglestone (12)
Rainham School for Girls

One Great Day . . .

On a coach, screams and shouts. Off the coach, not
excited. Looks at ride, worried, goes to ride, stares
into Jess' eyes. Jessica laughs, I'm shaking, scared.
It spun four times.
Laughed, smiled, water splashed into my face.
Make-up smudged, hair gone curly, we giggled.
Had a really good time

Chloe West (12)
Rainham School for Girls

259

I'm Late

I'm late, running to work, missed the bus. Oh no!
Dropped bag, picked it up, made it. Boss yelling,
calm down. At desk, tea break, coffee, finished work.
Time to go, caught the bus. Got home, made dinner.
Knife and fork, washing up. Time for bed.
Goodnight, sleep tight.

Effa Bailey (13)
Rainham School for Girls

Mr Ten-pence

1.1.07, I was born, a brand new ten-pence piece.
Shoved in a bag, road trip to Rainham. A till,
cramped, old ten-pences. Five minutes, a boy's hand,
small.
A purse, quite fancy!
A flying trip. I fell,
Oh no! A drain, cold, wet, *dead!*

Mea Bower (12)
Rainham School for Girls

Shop Tiff You Drop

Wake up, breakfast in bed. Order taxi, go to
Bluewater. Park the car. Shop around, Tammy, New
Look, many more. Tops, jeans, skirts galore.
Lunch time, café, salad, chicken. Go back home,
shopping bags. Have a bath, bed time. Really tired,
comfy bed.
Night-night, sleep tight.

Sarah Effiott (12)
Rainham School for Girls

Untitled

A new security guard took his position at the museum, to protect the rare ruby emerald from being stolen. a loud bang erupted, he sprinted down the corridors as fast as he could, but when he got there, the ruby emerald was gone.
He was too late, he had failed.

James Mason (14)
St Columba's School for Boys, Bexleyheath

Untitled

Walking down the road with the wind in my hair and the birds chirping. Total tranquillity. It's what makes my area nice. Everyone gets along with smiles all around.
Once I had finished reading the billboard, I just wished that it could come true. That crime would completely stop!

George Odd (14)
St Columba's School for Boys, Bexleyheath

Rush Hour

Alone, sitting. A stranger comes up to me and asks
me where the train station is. I say up the road on
the left and he says thanks and leaves.
I sat alone for 2 minutes, by myself and thought
about my life and my amazing wife and kids.
Boom!

Adam Orridge (14)
St Columba's School for Boys, Bexleyheath

265

Untitled

Luke was woken up, in his ground floor flat, by the beeping of his alarm. He waved his hand over the table with the annoying alarm clock on it and repeatedly pushed down the snooze button, but still the beeping continued. Then suddenly … a lorry came reversing into his room!

Dan Morris
St Columba's School for Boys, Bexleyheath

Untitled

John peeled back the page of the Nuts magazine, glanced around to see if anyone was looking. He couldn't let anyone know his dirty habit. He counted back the pages: one, two, three. It was the right thickness, so he began to clean the dirt from under his toenails.

George Roast (14)
St Columba's School for Boys, Bexleyheath

John's Situation

John was in a sticky situation. His girlfriend gave him a choice, he gives up his Xbox or she leaves. He thought really hard and decided to give up his Xbox, until he saw the advert for Techno3. His choice quickly changed and he said goodbye to Maria.

Harvey Lewis (14)
St Columba's School for Boys, Bexleyheath

The Escape

A deafening screech filled the entire mansion. I released the torch from my grip in utter fear of this horrific noise. I began to hear echoing footsteps, drawing ever closer. I grasped my knife firmly, as I had anticipated this might occur, and sprinted in search of an escape.

Oliver Moir (13)
St Columba's School for Boys, Bexleyheath

Untitled

The room was full of people with angry looks on their faces. They were hot and tired and the tension increased as another minute went by. The people were waiting to be told that their flight was ready to board.

Suddenly, they were told their flights had been delayed. *Again!*

William West (14)
St Columba's School for Boys, Bexleyheath

Untitled

We'd got out the Bunsen burners in science. The room's attention turned from the teacher to myself. I therefore turned the Bunsen burner off. In doing so I felt my blood rush up to my face in embarrassment, and I felt extraordinarily warm. It was my hair …
It was alight!

Donatien Mutarambirwa (14)
St Columba's School for Boys, Bexleyheath

271

Untitled

A boy was playing football. He started off as a sub and came on in the second half. All the players walked away from him, including his own team.
The referee went up to him and said, 'Are those pink slippers?'
He looked at everyone and they all laughed loudly.

Christopher Juff (14)
St Columba's School for Boys, Bexleyheath

The Death Of A Dear Pet

It was a cold Sunday morning, I woke up to the sight of my mother standing beside my bed. I wasn't sure what was wrong with her. She didn't look happy. Mother sat down beside me and said, 'I'm sorry, your pet rabbit's died.'

Anthony Walker (14)
St Columba's School for Boys, Bexleyheath

Untitled

Screeching around the corner came burning, black
tyres, with menacing faces behind the wheel. They
stared at their prey like predators.
The boy ran, looking back with sweat dripping down
his face into his eyes. His feet pumped but missed as
they passed the finish line, he stopped annoyingly.

Stuart Monaghan (14)
St Columba's School for Boys, Bexleyheath

Untitled

Adam woke to a banging on his door. He knew who it was, so he ignored it and went back to sleep. But the thunderous banging got louder. His door was creaking. He nervously walked to the door, he opened it to find a black eye in the morning.

Nick Joel (14)
St Columba's School for Boys, Bexleyheath

275

Untitled

In primary school, I was playing football when I slipped over and hit my head on the hard, cold floor. I went to the office and I was all drowsy and I could see stars. I had to go to the hospital and I had concussion. It really badly hurt!

Shane Dunphy
St Columba's School for Boys, Bexleyheath

The Cold Morning Going To School

I was riding in the misty morning, when a cold breeze passed me as the traffic lights turned green. I turned the corner and there was blood on the road. Its mouth was as dark as a tunnel, its feet were twitching, it was smelly.
It was a squirrel.

Charlie Corr

St Columba's School for Boys, Bexleyheath

Stuck In A Lift

It all goes black, I'm stuck, I can't see a thing. I'm on
my own in the dark. I reach for anything I can find
and *beep!*
'Hello, how can I help?' the soothing voice, calming
my beating heart.
'I'm stuck,' I gasped, 'I'm stuck in a lift.'
Heellpp!

Fraser Goddard
St Columba's School for Boys, Bexleyheath

And They Call It Puppy Love

'She likes you.'

'Really? Do you think?'

'Yeah, 'course! What do you think of her?'

'She's really cute.'

'That's what Gary said.'

'Not surprised, how can you tell that she likes me?'

'Well, if she likes someone she normally wags her tail and rolls over.'

'Oh.'

'Yeah … she hates Gary.'

Gavin Jordan
St Columba's School for Boys, Bexleyheath

Macro At Night

Where has Dad gone? There's no one in sight!
A door slams! Complete silence! Something smells
of fish. No wonder, I'm beside the fish stall, thinking
of what to do. Now I'm really scared, noises coming
from the far end of the gigantic store. Someone's
coming … a shadow approaching.

Joseph Franklin
St Columba's School for Boys, Bexleyheath

House Of Mirrors

I walk in, carefree. Suddenly I'm lost, all I can see is me. Me 500 times. I know one is a door, but which one?
I've been in here for fifteen minutes, this isn't fun anymore. When and how will I get out?
At last I find it, the door.

Ciaran Bridges
St Columba's School for Boys, Bexleyheath

Trapped In The Industry

'Huh? Where am I?'
This uncanny man telling me what to do. Telling me
to go out and purchase these things, then go off and
sell them to the public.
I am then in this peculiar room. That man rambles on
about how I'm not up to scratch …
'You're fired!'

Alex Turner
St Columba's School for Boys, Bexleyheath

Accident

'Catch,' he said.
I failed. I went to retrieve the ball but it was out of
my reach, so I leant on the greenhouse and … *smash!*
There was a hole, there was I in shock, ambulance
rushing and … I woke up. It was a dream.
Why does my arm hurt?

Joe Mulvihill
St Columba's School for Boys, Bexleyheath

283

The Statue

One statue on a grave, scared to show its face. Then
I blinked and it moved! Its eyes glowing red, pointing,
pointing to all the other statues.
I blinked again, all the statues moved. I ran for my
life. Did that statue really move?

Charley Robinson
St Columba's School for Boys, Bexleyheath

284

Goal, Or Is It?

The opposition's winning, everybody around him is
waiting for something special.
'We can win,' he screams.
He gets it, runs, people screaming, cheering,
jumping, he feels their eyes burning on him, like the
sun in summer. He shoots. It's about to hit the back
of the goal …
'Wake up!'

Chris Akinsanya
St Columba's School for Boys, Bexleyheath

Untitled

She was there, in front of me. She had me drooling
over her. I was introduced to her. I was working on
getting another girl, but I forgot about her.
I told myself, *get this girl!* I went to kiss her, but she
said, 'I have a boyfriend.'

David Akinuli
St Columba's School for Boys, Bexleyheath

Untitled

I'm at a sleepover, dreaming I'm kissing my wife; but
it's actually a mop. I've wet myself; everyone saw me
sleepwalk. I go back to sleep. I wake up to find out
that I was only daydreaming.
Everyone looking at me, because I was dribbling in
the English class!

Efimen Orukpe
St Columba's School for Boys, Bexleyheath

Spooky Night

I was 9 years old, I needed the toilet in the middle
of the night so I went, then I went to bed. Then the
toilet flushed so I got my pellet guns and stayed up
for the rest of the night.
Then it happened … I woke up!

Lee Manze
St Columba's School for Boys, Bexleyheath

Santa In Your Garden

Have you ever had Santa in your garden? He walks
on his tiptoes, sweating with fear that he might be
spotted. Suddenly he walks into the washing line.
Crash! Bang! Boom!
He falls to the floor with his black sack on top of him.
'Grandad, what are you doing?'

Jake Garth
St Columba's School for Boys, Bexleyheath

Falling

We started off together, then ended up apart. We started walking, suddenly it got too steep, I had to run. I was trying to stop myself. Then it happened, I started hurtling, stumbling, falling, with immense pain. Would I ever stop? I tried to help myself, but someone helped me …

Daniel Bermingham-Shaw
St Columba's School for Boys, Bexleyheath

Walking Through The Dark

Have you ever walked through the dark? You can't see what is around you. To be honest, I'm not scared of the dark. I'm scared of the monsters creeping through the dark.

Someone grabbed me, I started screaming. Wait a minute it was Samuel who grabbed me ...
Or something else!

Nathan Lewis

St Columba's School for Boys, Bexleyheath

The Great Escape

'Guys we're almost free, it won't be long until
Gigantor has sugar on his Weetabix.'
'Us coffee granules will be free from the cupboard.'
The cupboard suddenly opened. After what felt like
an eternity.
'Let's go, go, go, go, jump! We are free!'
Splat! Jamie stood on the coffee granules.

Nathan Syme (13)
Sir Roger Manwood's School

Spooked

As others boarded the coach, I was rushing into
the museum. Turning, I spotted my bag. But then
a transparent figure floated into view. Transfixed, I
stared straight through it as it removed its head from
under its arm, and threw it at me.
I forgot my bag and ran.

Joseph Wheeler (13)
Sir Roger Manwood's School

293

Fireworks!

The night drew to an end, the sounds of fireworks
dying out. Bright lights filled the sky as everyone
cheered. My family and I were having a great time,
suddenly a rocket hit a young boy. Loud screaming
filled the air, it reminded me of what happened to
Guy Fawkes!

Sade Carpenter (13)
Sir Roger Manwood's School

294

Cheeseboard Massacre

'Run, run!' said Stilton to Cheddar the cheese.
Stilton was dying. Cheese fondue leaked out of his
side. The knife went in for the final blow but the
cheese wasn't there.
Dougal the dog stood in the corner, licking his lips.
I couldn't resist that! he thought.

Fraser Newgreen (13)
Sir Roger Manwood's School

Wrong Impressions!

I was scared. The lights kept flickering on and off. I heard footsteps getting closer. *Tap, tap,* that's when they stopped. I ducked under the covers. The door creaked for a second, then swung open.
'Do you want a cookie?' said my mum with a smile, standing in my doorway.

Erin Clague (13)
Sir Roger Manwood's School

The 'Unwilling' Sleeping Beauty

The pyjamad zombies marched towards me. I froze.
There was no way out, although the castle walls did
have windows - no way could I jump!
'I don't want to become the 'Sleeping Beauty'. I don't
care what the legend says. Oh where is my knight in
shining armour? Help! *Argh!*'

Kate Spencer (13)

Sir Roger Manwood's School

Friday The 13th

It is Friday night, Friday the 13th. The streets are pitch-black. As I turn, shadows fade into the darkness. I'm not alone.

News presenter, 'Friday night a boy's carcass was left on the sidewalk in no name street. A message to everyone, do not go outside your house alone …'

Michael Forrister (13)
Sir Roger Manwood's School

The Danger Of Refereeing

Anger explodes from his body, his face turns as red as the card he has been shown. The referee orders him off the pitch. It only makes him worse. His teammates try to force him off, but he won't budge. He reaches the referee. One enormous punch! The ref's dead.

Jake Lamerton (13)
Sir Roger Manwood's School

Drink 'n' Drive

We exited the pub, Dad was completely drunk but that did not stop him driving.
'Eh, get in the car.'
I hesitated, but what would he do if I refused?
I jumped in the car regretting my every move. Then, suddenly there were two bright lights approaching us.
'Wake up!'

Jared Goodrich (12)
Sir Roger Manwood's School

300

Getting Even

I had a dog, fed it Whiskas, it bit me, went to hospital. The doctor said, infected with rabies. He went out, came back in, then says, 'Nice to see you're making a sorry letter.'
'Oh no,' I say, 'this is a list of people I'm gonna bite before dying!'

Ohifebo Edeki (12)
Sir Roger Manwood's School

The Wave

Salty sea air stinging my face. Hair, dripping wet
covering my eyes. The swell of the wave… I
paddle. The huge expanse of water envelopes me, a
monstrous cavern of pure adrenaline. For a moment
nothing else exists; time stops my mind clear. Then
Ire submerge. The bath's now cold!

Grace Thomas (12)
Sir Roger Manwood's School

The Chase

He pounced faster and faster with his tongue flapping out. People started to stop and stare for a while, it may have been my smell. I dived into a bush without him spotting me, then ran after him. As soon as he turned around, I knew it was over.
'Woof!'

Luke Smith (12)
Sir Roger Manwood's School

The Flight

The air hostess checked my ticket.
'To the left,' she said politely.
I was sitting between a thin man and a chubby
woman. The plane took off, the man was nervous,
he was tense. My chair shook rapidly, I was scared, I
looked, the lady had gone to the toilets.

Kristie Lee (12)
Sir Roger Manwood's School

A Bad Night Out

Smash! The boy scrambled through the car window.
'Get in!' he yelled to the other boys. They got in.
'Got the drink?' one asked.
'Yep.'
He revved the engine with his knife. They drove
off into the night, skidding and jolting, with yells of
excitement.
Crash! It all went silent.

Dominic Rees (12)
Sir Roger Manwood's School

305

Why My Mum's The Clumsiest Person In The World

This Christmas my mum said she would get everything right. She didn't. She fell over the dog and dropped the turkey all over the floor, she burnt all of the vegetables, she didn't think and chucked the dessert in the bin. Never mind, at least she didn't spill the gravy!

Alexandra Weaver (12)
Sir Roger Manwood's School

306

The Explosion

I was driving my car along the street when all of a sudden it cut out. I opened the bonnet, the engine was steaming out loads of smoke. I went to a car repair shop. They tried to help and my car blew up and the whole crew were dead.

Ryan Norton (12)
Sir Roger Manwood's School

The Chase

My opponent's breath beat down on my neck. My jog quickened into a sprint. I dodged trees and soon met the forest's edge. A pyramid? With no time to think, I dashed into pitch-black corridors. I didn't know what to do. Thank God it was only a computer game.

Esther Reed (12)
Sir Roger Manwood's School

All Alone

I was scared, it was dark, my cat was screaming outside. I froze. A spiked black figure crawled in front of me. Was it supernatural or a joke? The lights flickered on, my cat was sat before me, he had been chewing the electric wire outside. Oh no, vet bill.

Bethany-Rose White (12)
Sir Roger Manwood's School

309

The Suited City

I walk the streets of the city. I look left. I look right. I
look all around. Everywhere I see them. Men in suits.
Women in suits. Big people in suits. Small people in
suits. Everywhere are people in suits. People carrying
briefcases. People looking smart. The suited city.
London.

Evie Sparkes (12)
Sir Roger Manwood's School

My Journey Home

School was horrible today. Lost one of my shoes, dropped homework in a puddle, bag got stolen by dog. Went to the train station, dropped other shoe on track! On train standing near old man smoking, got off, walked along a strange street, I'd got off; at the wrong place!

Hugh Jones (11)
Sir Roger Manwood's School

311

Ouch!

I was going along, just minding my own business when … *bang!* I had fallen off the swing! People came running over asking if I was alright. They helped me up and went on their way.
Ouch! That really hurt! Oh, it was only me falling out of my bed.

Vicki Bee (11)
Sir Roger Manwood's School

My Present

I couldn't wait as I flew down the stairs. I had been
up all night too excited to sleep.
What could it be? I thought. *A computer game, a gift
voucher or just money?*
I scrambled to unwrap it. But no, not what I thought,
a gigantic hand-knitted jumper.

Emma Marsh (12)
Sir Roger Manwood's School

Money

A boy had saved up for a wide-screen TV. He washed cars, made lemonade, cleaned houses, and more. He now had £390 and to get the TV he needed £400. So he stole £10 from a girl.
He went to the shop and they said, 'Sorry we've sold out!'

Emile Heywood (12)
Sir Roger Manwood's School

Running

I kept running, sweat trickled down my face. There!
An alley! I turned in. The two policemen ran by,
unaware of my hiding place. I turned. A man stood
behind me! In his hand was - *'Argh!'* I screamed.
Colour faded from my sight.
I later awoke in a hospital bed.

Jack Butcher (12)
Sir Roger Manwood's School

A Dream?

He was panting. He couldn't go on any further.
Suddenly there was a huge bang. Everything went
black but he could still hear his own breath.
He tried to stand up, but his muscles wouldn't obey
him. He felt completely paralysed.
He suddenly woke. It must have been a dream.

Omar Tarmohamed (12)
Sir Roger Manwood's School

316

Poodle Pie

I hate my wife. She looks so old. We both are now,
but she is always shouting at me and loving that dog
instead of me. That's why I had to do it.
'Where is my dinner?' she shouts again.
'Here it is darling, poodle pie. Enjoy!'

Offie Briscall-Harvey (11)
Sir Roger Manwood's School

The Lucky Pen

One day I found a really nice pen when it was raining hard. Suddenly the rain stopped. I thought the pen was lucky. My mum said she'd bought me a nice new car. The pen really was lucky. Until I found out that it was a toy car! Just typical!

William Sim (12)
Sir Roger Manwood's School

318

The Crash Fall

I knew I couldn't get the plane to land on the beach.
The island was too small. Crashed against a rock.
Who sabotaged the plane? Someone coming. Must
hide. Cave over there. It's slippery in here. Where is
the entrance? Help! *Whack!* Heelp!

Brendan Kjellberg-Motton (11)
Sir Roger Manwood's School

Murder In The Alley

Stale death hung in the air. My watch read 12.07.
President Putin lay, face down in the mud, a knife
stuck in his back, surrounded by a sea of blood.
Typical M25 traffic. I was just too late. The murderer
was gone. Escaped to the world outside.

Thomas Ashley (13)
Sir Roger Manwood's School

Ice Cream!

'He is here Luke,' said Marley. 'The ice cream man won't wait forever.'
Luke rushed to the van.
'Je voudrais deux glace au chocolat,' Luke asked the man. Of course they were in France.
Luke took the ice creams from the man.
'Merci, beaucoup Monsieur,' Luke said, thankfully, walking away.

Luke Lindhurst (13)
Sir Roger Manwood's School

321

The Vampire's Pet

I didn't know what to do! The vampire stood over
him waiting for his newt's poison to kick in. I made
the choice, I would take the place of my best friend.
'If you cure him,' I muttered, 'I will accept your offer.'
The vampire smiled thinly. He looked menacingly.

Curtis Maidens (13)
Sir Roger Manwood's School

Stupid

Mr Smith went to the hospital, he came out really happy because he had his sight back. He got on the train to go home. Mr Smith killed himself on the train, why?
Because he went through a tunnel and thought he had lost his sight again!

Ella Savage (13)
Sir Roger Manwood's School

The End Of The World

'It's the end of the world tomorrow,' said George.
'Oh right, that's cool,' I replied.
So that night I went out, I spent all my money and
had fun, I went wild! I went to bed expecting the end
of the world to come. Sadly it never came.

Amy Lewis-Gafer (13)
Sir Roger Manwood's School

Detective Mystery

Mr Winter lay on the floor in a pool of blood. He was dead. An iron pole lay on the floor next to him and a gust of wind blew through the open window through which the murderer had escaped.
Detective Smith arrived at the scene. He was too late.

Reece Creedon (12)
Sir Roger Manwood's School

Into Space We Go!

Incoming android! Watch out. Outer space seems so far away when you're battling with characters, similar to the ones in Star Wars. Here we go, we are just about to hit the black hole! Wow! It's like falling into a bad dream then falling back out again. Back to reality.

Alex Chadwick (13)
Sir Roger Manwood's School

Swimming Race

'Take your marks, go,' shouted the starter.
I dived into the icy cold water. I did three massive fly kicks as I rose to the surface.
Twenty quick stream-lined strokes, I took before I reached the end. I looked up at the timing board, and couldn't believe I'd won.

Dominika Szucsova (13)
Sir Roger Manwood's School

327

The Accident

'Argh!' he cried. He was crumpled up on the pavement.
'You'll be alright,' strangers told him.
The sirens could be heard coming closer. He told the ambulance paramedic something. The paramedics tried their best but he later died.
The something was, 'I would rather die than live with my mum!'

Jacob Dobbs (13)
Sir Roger Manwood's School

Who's In The Dark?

The clock read 11.52. *Bang!* The front door slammed tight. Stairs old and creaking. My heart started pumping blood at 100mph. I reached under my bed and slowly pulled the 'bat for emergencies' free. Tiptoeing across my room, I heaved my bedroom door wide open. Muffled scream! It's Mum!

Moffy Little (13)
Sir Roger Manwood's School

Limbo

The mall. That's where I was. When it happened. I saw him. The hand in pocket. The glint of metal. The loud bang. The searing pain.
I'm in a pain-free place now. Not Heaven or Hell. Black. Pure black. Limbo. That's where I am. While they decide my fate.

Laura Gibson (13)
Sir Roger Manwood's School

The Man

I watched the second hand crawl around to the twelve. He should be here by now. I picked up the phone and held it to my ear. It was dead. Suddenly the electricity failed. I lit a candle. There was a knock. I opened the door and screamed.

Viv Hayfes (13)
Sir Roger Manwood's School

Edward And Tedward

'Eddy, Eddy,' Tedward cried.
Tedward was Edward's favourite teddy bear. They
told each other everything. But Edward's dragon-lady
mum had stuffed Tedward in a dark box in the attic.
Light filled the box and there stood Eddy.
'Tedward, I'll never let you go,' cried Edward.
Edward had saved Tedward.

Brooke Miffar (13)
Sir Roger Manwood's School

332

The Match

Jerry sat down to watch television. His parents had gone to bed. Nothing good was on television, Jerry was bored, then he remembered the matches. He set one alight and watched the fire dance. The fire licked Jerry's fingers, and he dropped the match. The house was engulfed by flames.

Henry Smith (13)
Sir Roger Manwood's School

The Bus Journey

A man got onto a bus that goes in a circle. He got on the bus and fell asleep. When he woke up he was only one stop from home. He went and punched the driver because he thought he had gone slowly. But he had already gone round once!

Oliver Sanford (13)
Sir Roger Manwood's School

Grease Ball

The popular girls were laughing at me again. I'd had
enough of it. This had been going on too long.
'Grease ball,' they called me, along with, 'Rapunzel.'
I went to the loos and took the scissors out of my
pencil case. I held up my long hair, and cut.

Anna Preston (12)
Sir Roger Manwood's School

Intensive Care

We were silent until we got on the motorway.
Georgina was constantly nagging me to overtake and
indicate, what a backseat driver.
Whilst telling Georgina to shut up I lost control of
the car. We swerved and hit another car which hit
the rails, spinning, screaming, twirling, tumbling and
dying.

William French (12)
Sir Roger Manwood's School

Flying And Soaring

The eagle soars high over the mountain tops. His keen eyes watching over his territory. Suddenly he spots a bird, a sparrow, far below. Slowly, secretly, he drops. *Bam!* He slams into the sparrow and sends it spiralling to the ground. He carries on and thinks, *another day, another death*.

Sam Barons (13)
Sir Roger Manwood's School

The Dragon

My knife was drawn, it glinted in the moonlight. A branch broke, it wasn't me! The roar echoed through the trees. I spun round, to my horror it was there. I threw my knife, it did nothing.
It knocked me back and I fell into eternal darkness, never to return.

Daniel Starling (13)
The Harvey Grammar School

Clones

On the gunship I felt safe. Outside the gunship,
scared. We felt a rumble, gunship went down.
'Take cover.' We did. Our army was three times
larger than the enemy's. They were getting
destroyed by snipers.
I woke, up-wires were being replaced by health
androids!

Lee Mitcheff (13)
The Harvey Grammar School

339

Graduation Day

1,000 eyes bore into me, some of them are laughing,
others are crying. I just stare. It is the end, yet the
beginning. I walk that never-ending walk until …
'Congratulations.'
'Thank you Sir.'
I grin that most famous grin and … It is done, I am
finally free. Graduation day!

Sherif Attia (13)
The Harvey Grammar School

Abyss

He jumped into the abyss and then he was under the water. The sheer heat caused him to gasp and struggle to the surface. When he finally got up, he choked on the water and nearly threw up. Then his mum shouted, 'Bob is round, get out of that sauna!'

Joshua Caruana (13)
The Harvey Grammar School

The End

There were monkeys, jumping madly, crows shouting
loudly, raging lions, penguins falling over, my brother
… asleep. There was a wild beast. My mother wide
awake. The snake scaly and green.
Then along came the shark, big and mean, a pure
killing machine. It came and attacked.
Television turned black!

Aman Tariq (13)
The Harvey Grammar School

The Deep End

I was standing on the edge. I could feel the adrenaline pumping. There just wasn't any point anymore. My father had driven me to this. But then, this was my job, I got paid to swim long distances. I dived and swam to the finish.

Jordan Saviff (13)
The Harvey Grammar School

The Snowball

He glanced over my shoulder, eyes of fire burning with intent, as if he was just about to kill me. My mirror caught sight of his deadly weapon. Small in size but in the right hands, very dangerous. He whipped his hand round and hit me with the snowball!

Peter Harris (13)
The Harvey Grammar School

Beast

Blood. It ran down my bedraggled body. The beast
was winning. I staggered to the beast, blade ready.
I lunged aggressively at the startled beast, knocking
it off its feet. It screamed, trying to alleviate its pain.
Slowly and carefully, it refreshed in its screams of
agony … so I thought.

Oliver Webb (13)
The Harvey Grammar School

Creak

'What was that?'
'I don't know, maybe it was your brain rattling
around!'
'Very funny.' *Creak.* 'There it is again.'
'I heard it that time.' The creaking came closer and
closer. A dark hand poked around the door.
'Who's there?' No answer.
I said, 'Who's there?'
'Don't worry, it's me.'

James Waddoups (13)
The Harvey Grammar School

When Robots Attack

Last night I was walking down the street and a shiny object attacked me. I tried to kick it but it hurt my foot. I picked up a pole and hit the object. After I went to inspect it, I found out it was a prototype NASA robot.

Alex Zerbino (13)
The Harvey Grammar School

347

Death

Screaming woke me from my slumber and I stared through my front windscreen, but too late did I realise my danger. My car vaulted over the barrier, darkness surrounded me. Warmth spread through my limbs and around my face. I felt tired and slowly, silence re-established its vast empire.

James Cooper (13)
The Harvey Grammar School

Freefall

I tripped, falling, falling. I was certainly doomed. My
hair was milky white from where I hit the chalk.
Reaching the end of my journey, I prayed.
I scrunched my eyes tightly and tucked into a ball ... I
screamed.
I woke later, I had landed in a roofless, pillow truck.

Stuart Walsh (13)
The Harvey Grammar School

349

Demon King

A cold wave of nausea swept over me, leaving me completely immobilised. I knew demons were scary, but this was beyond reality.
'Ephraim, help would be nice.'
That returned me to the land of the living. Tightening my grip on the lance I began to run towards the Demon King.

Samuel Bailey (13)
The Harvey Grammar School

350

The Monster

I heard that dreaded sound, I bolted, taking the steps three at a time. I skidded round a corner and sailed out the kitchen window. I rounded a corner when, a shadow loomed in front of me.

There was no escape from Dad and my school report!

Josh Rawlings (13)
The Harvey Grammar School

I'm The Target

It was swooping down towards me. I could feel the
adrenaline rush inside me. Its tip was slicing through
the air, not stopping until it hit its target.
It got me right in the eye. That damned paper
aeroplane!

James Thwaites (13)
The Harvey Grammar School

Shattered

He rides his horse, determined for revenge. A sweet feeling of victory rushes through his arms and legs as he gallops away. He enters the battlefield, sees the enemy ready as ever. Attack! They close into him and smash, a blow of the sword and his dreams are shattered.

Bashishta Gaire (13)
The Harvey Grammar School

Crash Landing

The aeroplane started to dip, it was going to have to crash land into the dark cave ahead. The hand-like creature gripped harder on the tail and the pilot lost control totally. He could see the stalagmites and stalactites looming.

Yuck, thought the baby, *I hate baby food*.

Herbie Tyler (13)
The Harvey Grammar School

My Bravery Award

I caught this villain, it all happened when he was
being chased by the police. He ditched his car and
ran my way. I tackled him to the ground.
I now have a bravery award and I'm training to be a
police officer.

William O'Donnell (13)
The Harvey Grammar School

Disaster Ride

I was on, bars and pads all around me. We were
about to go, and then we were off!
Blurred vision, breathing harder and harder. Up we
went into space and raced back down again and
again. We suddenly came to an abrupt halt. We were
stuck!

Matthew Greene (13)
The Harvey Grammar School

The Rush

Suddenly I was rushing through the air at high speed, straight towards a rock face! I tried to turn and slow down, but nothing worked. Nothing could stop the blindingly fast journey to death.
Then I woke up …

Aidan Fudge (13)
The Harvey Grammar School

Untitled

It was coming down, rapidly, splattering on the ground as it hit. No people were around, apart from the few standing under the roofs. There was me soaked, in the middle of the street.
After waiting for some minutes I got in, it then stopped …

Joel Dix (13)
The Harvey Grammar School

The Noise

I woke up and heard a noise. I headed downstairs
with a baseball bat. I went into the kitchen, but
nothing stirred. So I went into the cellar and found a
large nest of birds, but that wasn't the noise.
I found a sleepwalking girl!

Jamie Crouch (13)
The Harvey Grammar School

World War One

My Sergeant screamed, 'Wake up!' I got up and went
to my sniper position. Immediately people started
firing at me, they were English.
I shouted, 'Why are you shooting at me?'
Someone replied, 'You have a Nazi flag on your face
and are wearing a German uniform.'
It was true!

Karl Lynch (12)
The Harvey Grammar School

PlayStation

He punched and punched, my nose was bleeding. He got in a car and left me for dead. The police chased after him and forced him over a cliff. I heard sounds of gunshots as the man fell, dead. Then I turned off my PlayStation and went up to bed.

Mitchell Bloomfield (13)
The Harvey Grammar School

The Date That Never Happened

John jumped into his car and accelerated to his date
with a beautiful and charming girl. He dreamt about
how the date was going to go.
As he approached the meeting point, he sped up.
Suddenly, a girl stepped into the road, the date was
over before it had begun.

Michael Winstanley (13)
The Harvey Grammar School

362